# THE ORPHAN NURSE

AUDREY BARLOW

# PROLOGUE

$\mathcal{C}$harles was gone less than an hour when they heard a commotion outside, right at their doorstep. Mary ran to look, Anne fast behind. He stood with two men holding each arm, his eyes wide, terrified. Anne gasped and reached for him, too far to grab.

'What is it? Why, what have you done?'

Charles shook his head. 'Nothing! I've done nothing wrong. Please, Anne. Tell them,' he said, desperate. Tommy watched from a corner, thumb in his mouth. 'Anne! Tell them!'

'Let him go!' was all she managed.

One of the men laughed. 'Caught red-handed. Theft's the charge. Don't see him coming home soon.' Charles said something else, lost under the angry sounds, under Anne's scream and Mary's rising cry.

'Don't take my father! Don't!'

Their voices followed him down the street, joined by others – a sea of wives and children, gathering round the scene. Some faces she knew, some she'd never seen, but they all had the same prying look. Charles could only shake his head as the men dragged him along. A constable joined them, urging them on. Charles tried to speak, mouth open, saying the same thing over and over again. 'Please.'

Anne stood, wooden, her eyes following the scene as it faded into the murk of the evening. Her lips moved as if in prayer, but there were no words that Mary could hear. She watched Anne as much as she watched Charles, fearing her mother would crumble into pieces if she took her eyes away.

One woman stepped up to Anne, grabbing her arm. 'He'll be let go soon,' she said. 'They just like making a fuss.' But her voice didn't believe itself. She had a baby in one arm, and the child reached towards Anne's neck, pulling at the chain with the cross. That was all they had left.

Mary grabbed her mother's hand, tugging her back inside, leaving the woman's words like dust in the air.

Mary and Tommy trailed behind, holding on to each other, holding onto anything but the truth.

By the time they returned to their rooms, Anne sank to the floor, whispering to herself as Mary pulled her along. 'Theft? Not my Charles. Never my Charles.'

'I'll go to Mr Turner,' Mary said, forcing the words out. 'He can fix it. He must fix it.'

'Go. Go, girl. Go and get your father. Bring him home.'

Mary did as she was told, legs burning as she sprinted through the streets, through the late-night walkers and hawkers. Through the eyes that stared at her as she ran. She didn't stop. She couldn't stop.

# CHAPTER 1

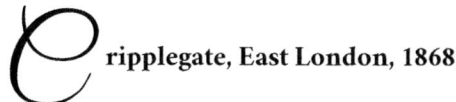ripplegate, East London, 1868.

Mary Bennett, barely twelve but feeling twice as old, pushed back her tangled hair and watched a droplet of candle wax slither across the table. It skittered dangerously close to the tower of dirty dishes before plopping to the floor, where Tommy had drawn an untidy scrawl of stick figures.

'Look at that,' her four-year-old brother crowed, 'they're drowning!' His eyes were alive with mischief, and his mouth was stained with the jam they'd eaten for supper.

At the grate, her mother nursed a small flame, coaxing it into life with tender breaths. The flickering light stressed her thinness, her beauty swallowed by exhaustion, but when she turned to Mary and Tommy, she offered a smile that spoke of warmth.

'If you're finished drawing, help clear the table before your father gets in.'

But Tommy was racing to the window, flinging open the

curtains to let in a dimness thick with fog and chimney smoke.

'I see him!' he shouted, bouncing with glee.

Charles Bennett tapped on the glass and gave them a grin that belied his weariness, then paused in the doorway, shaking the damp from his coat.

'Home at last!'

Tommy leapt into his arms, clinging like a monkey. 'Got a good hold, have you?' He swung the boy up and around, setting him down with a gentle thud before reaching for Mary. She held back a little, catching the blue tinge under his eyes, the gauntness of his cheeks.

'You're wet, Father.'

'Not half as wet as them sailors. You'd think I was made of sugar the way you're worrying. It won't melt me.' He kissed her forehead and moved to Anne, who enveloped him in an embrace. They all huddled together, a cocoon of warmth against the world's harshness beyond their four walls, until Tommy wriggled free and danced around them.

'Are we going to eat? I'm starved!'

'Just like a man,' said Anne, her eyes crinkling with amusement. 'Go on, you two. Fetch the plates.'

Mary and Tommy dashed to the table, barely dodging each other in the cramped space. They grabbed the dishes, bumping and laughing, while Charles rubbed his hands near the newly lit fire. 'Bless you, Anne. I'd never make it without you.'

They gathered round the table, Charles with a fresh towel around his neck and Tommy with crumbs already strewn across his shirt. The meal was sparse: bread and a sliver of cheese, tea steeped so long it was almost black. But there was comfort in the ritual, the way Anne poured the tea just so, the way Charles broke the bread and passed it with a nod. They ate with the hunger of those who knew want and did not fear it, filling their stomachs and hearts with each other's company.

Tommy chattered without pause, his tales of the day's adventures veering wildly from reality. Mary listened with half an ear, her mind flitting to her books, her dreams, the murmur of a world beyond the grey confines of their life. She stole a glance at her father, saw him watching her with an amused twinkle. 'You've grown quiet, Mary. Not like most twelve-year-olds I know. Planning a grand escape?'

'No,' she replied, a faint smile tugging at her lips. 'Just wondering about things.'

'What sort of things?'

Mary hesitated, fiddling with the edge of her cup. She knew her questions would sound foolish, but they pressed at her, relentless. 'Does everyone work as hard as you do?'

Charles chuckled, a sound rich with love. 'It's the way of the world, lass. No one gets by without a fight. But I'm a lucky man. Got my family. Got my health. And I have Mr Turner looking out for me. We should all be grateful.'

Mary shifted in her chair. She'd never met John Turner, but felt his presence. She had no words to explain her apprehension, so she nodded and picked at her bread, trying to mould her thoughts into silence.

Charles leaned back. 'It's a blessing he's the overseer. You should have seen him with Davey Wilson, giving him an advance payment when their little lad took ill. Never seen a man so thankful. Even the doctor thought there was no chance. It's a miracle what he did. God's own miracle.'

His voice brimmed with sincerity, but it only added to Mary's confusion. The picture painted by her father was one of generosity, yet she felt a discordant note that she couldn't ignore. 'I'm sure Mr Turner is very kind.' She didn't want to upset him. Not after a long night of hauling crates and dodging foremen's shouts.

Tommy had abandoned his meal to draw boats and fish across the table. Mary nudged him with her elbow, sending his pencil skittering to the floor.

'Oi, that's not fair!'

'It's not fair to mess up my work, either. Come on, help me with these before you drown the whole kitchen.' She stacked the plates high. He followed her lead, skipping away from their parents, who lingered at the fire's edge, whispering of things too adult for young ears.

'Mary.' It was Anne's voice. 'What's wrong, love?'

'Nothing.'

Anne glanced at Charles, then back to Mary. 'We know you better than that. Something's troubling you.'

The truth wavered on Mary's lips. She longed to spill her fears, her worries, but they felt unformed and childish. 'I just want Father to be careful.'

'Careful?' Charles sounded baffled but tender. 'No one's careful on the docks. If we started now, it would be chaos. Best not worry yourself.'

But worry was all Mary could do. She carried it like a cloak, wrapping herself in doubt even as she longed to cast it off.

'There's that Sunday picnic they're planning for us. A fortnight from now. Mr Turner's organising the whole thing, I hear. Food and games. Everyone's saying what a grand day it'll be.'

'Aye,' Anne said. 'You wouldn't be surprised to hear, but Mrs Wilson told me this morning...'

It was an opening they all knew well. Charles winked at Mary. 'If Mrs Wilson said it, you can count on it being true. You know her way with news.'

Tommy seized his chance to leave the dishes behind, running back to the warm comfort of his father's side. 'What did she say? What did she say?'

'She said you're a troublesome monkey and a great torment,' Charles said, mussing Tommy's hair. 'Nothing new there.'

The evening stretched thin and cosy around them. They'd cleared away the remnants of supper, Anne bustling with the tidying as Charles regaled them with tales of the day's work. The rough language of the docks softened by his fondness for storytelling. He poked fun at Mary, shaking his head with mock disbelief. 'You'd think someone had bigger plans,' he said, 'than dreaming of...'

Mary's voice cut him off. 'I'm going to be a nurse, Father. I told you already.'

'Not so fast! Who'll run the house with me gone and you off saving lives?'

Anne laughed. 'Leave the poor girl alone, Charles. You'll make her too important for us if you're not careful.'

Mrs Wilson arrived then, an untimely but welcome guest. She bustled in like she owned the place, her eyes bright with news. 'There you are,' she said, depositing herself near the fire, where she was free to stir the pot of their lives with knowing abandon. 'Did you hear about the Sidneys? About Lucy and that dreadful cough of hers?' She leaned closer to Anne. 'Awful business, it is.'

'It's been doing its round. Charles's hardly sleeping at all, with the work and the worry.'

'Terrible,' Mrs Wilson tutted sympathetically. 'Anyway, remember that picnic I mentioned this morning? The families are talking of nothing else. Turner's really outdone himself this time.'

Mary wanted to be impressed by the news. She was. And yet. Yet. She couldn't quiet the noise in her heart.

# CHAPTER 2

The day opened to reveal more of the same. Grey and wet, a shroud that hung low and thick, waiting to be pierced by another drop of rain. Charles had already gone, kissed them each in their beds before trudging out into the mist.

They did what they always did in his absence. It wasn't enough to fill the hours until he returned. Anne mended things that barely held together. Tommy wriggled and jostled and agitated against the dim routine. Mary dreamed, awake and asleep, as was her way. She imagined other lives, other futures.

She decided, finally, that they must see him. If they waited, the day would eat them whole. 'Come on, Tommy. Let's fetch Father at the docks.'

'It's a long way,' Anne protested mildly. 'The streets are a mess. And that boy will wear you out before you get there.'

'He's not so hard to catch.' Mary tugged at his arm, prompting a squeal and a happy chase through the kitchen. 'We'll be careful. And we won't be late. I promise.'

Tommy whooped his delight. No further convincing was

required. Anne relented with a smile and a wave. 'Take his hat. And yours. I don't want you catching your deaths.'

They pulled their hats low and their collars high, battling the wind as it kicked up their skirts and scattered Tommy's laughter. It was a miserable walk, but their excitement and Tommy's ceaseless enthusiasm made it bearable. The promise of their father's face at the end, his pride in them braving the elements, warmed them in ways their thin coats couldn't.

The streets were swollen with muck and people. Dirty water ran in rivulets, sweeping the day and its miseries past those too weary to avoid it. No one lingered outside longer than need demanded. Mary caught their hurried glimpses as she dodged Tommy's antics. She saw exhaustion and purpose, endless work. She saw futures that no one dreamed about, not like hers.

Near the docks, the world took on a new kind of energy. Workers and carriages bustled in a great frenzy, unloading crates and voices in equal measure. It was loud and full of desperate purpose. Mary had been a hundred times, but the sheer scale of it still left her dizzy and overwhelmed.

'Which way is he? Is he done? Is he here?' Tommy bounced like a toy sprung from its box. He darted around and through and past the chaos, a narrow flash of joyful madness. Mary struggled to keep up, to see past the throng and find a path through the crush.

'Slow down! I'm not as quick as you.'

But Tommy had already disappeared in the crowd, and she called his name in panic. Then she saw him, at a distance, nearly colliding with a tall man who stooped low and caught him before he could bolt again. Tommy wasn't afraid. He was nothing but delighted. The man was patiently listening to the child's excited chatter about his toys and drawings. The man's authority was clear even from a distance – dock workers passed him respectfully, touching their caps. Mary knew at once who it was.

As she approached, he looked at her with an amused but genuine smile, and she flushed with uncertainty and her long trek through the damp. 'You must be Mary,' he said, extending a hand. 'Your father speaks of you often. A clever girl, if he's to be believed. I suspect you already know me, but allow me to introduce myself.'

'Mr Turner,' she replied politely.

'And you found your way to the docks? I'm impressed.'

She clutched Tommy's arm, keeping him close. He squirmed against her grip.

'I brought him,' Mary explained. 'I brought him to see Father.'

Turner nodded with an expression that bordered on fatherly, and she thought, perhaps, that she'd imagined her reluctance. He was kind and pleasant and seemed genuinely interested. Her father was right. Her mother, too. He was as they said.

The man regarded them both, taking measure of their smallness against the scope of his work and the sweep of the day. He lowered his voice, though the bustling chaos all around swallowed most of his words. 'I'm glad you've come,' he told them. 'I hoped for a chance to speak to you. I'm very fond of your father. He works hard, and he's loyal. That's rare. I expect good things for him.'

'You do?'

'I do. He doesn't know it yet, but I'm considering him for a position. One with better pay. One where his skills might be better applied. I have great hopes.'

Her heart raced. They'd only ever known hard work and uncertainty. To have that changed, so suddenly and inexplicably. It was too much to imagine, and she was afraid to embrace it too easily.

Tommy, fearless and unbothered by the weight of things, whooped his glee. 'Did you hear that? Mary, did you hear that? Da is the best man on the docks. Mr Turner said so!' He spun in happy circles around the man's legs, unaware of Mary's silence and internal confusion.

She wanted to believe it. More than anything. Her father deserved it.

Turner chuckled, clearly enjoying Tommy's exuberance. 'You must promise not to spoil the surprise. Let me tell him in my own time. In my own way. Can you do that?'

Tommy nodded, not to be deterred. Mary hesitated. Her hopes washed away her certainty of doubt. She nodded too.

They made their way back through the docks. Turner had pointed them in the right direction, where they'd find Charles with no trouble. He'd told her more than she'd known before, but not enough. She couldn't hold the ideas in her head all at once.

Charles greeted them with broad astonishment, unable to hide his pride in them. 'Did you come all the way in this weather? You should have let me fetch you.'

'Tommy ran half the way,' said Mary, breathless and exhausted. 'Mother won't believe it.'

'Then I'll have to carry you both home on my back.' Charles swung Tommy up and reached for Mary, taking in the wonder on her face. He hoisted her up, balancing them both.

'We saw Mr Turner!' Tommy yelled. 'He's going to give you...'

Mary interrupted him. 'We promised we wouldn't tell.'

Charles shook his head, amused by the secrecy. 'And whose bright idea was that? Yours?'

'His,' Mary replied. 'But I think it's a good one.'

The walk home felt lighter, despite the rain and their growing fatigue. Mary's thoughts were thick and strange with hope. Perhaps her misgivings had been the wild ideas of a girl too eager to doubt. Or perhaps they were right. She wouldn't know until the future played itself out. She wouldn't know until they stood, alone and together, against the changing world.

# CHAPTER 3

The Bennett home, usually so grim, seemed to shine with hope as Mary tied her brother's worn laces and kissed him on the head. 'Tommy! Don't let them get too close now,' she called after him, her voice soft with a new optimism. Her father stood in the corner. 'Our luck's about to turn,' he said.

'It's Mr Turner, Charles! He must be the Lord's own angel.'

Charles clasped his wife's hand, and together they danced around the table, giddy with the promise of brighter days. 'The theatre!' Anne exclaimed, already dreaming aloud. 'And new boots for you, Mary. School again! We can have a proper Sunday supper!' She touched the cross around her neck. 'Oh, how I knew the Lord would provide for us.' Charles caught Mary by the waist and twirled her around with him, his energy unstoppable.

'You're all flush with foolishness!' Mary laughed, surprised at her own laughter. The dull grey of their two rooms seemed warmer, alive with joy. It had been years since she'd seen her father so free of worry. 'Mr Turner did well by you, didn't he, Father?' she said, trying to join in their jubilation.

'Our Charles,' Anne said. 'Foreman!'

'Dock foreman today, captain tomorrow. You mark me, girls; we'll be in the West End in no time!' He lifted Anne's chin, kissing her lips softly, a gesture that Mary couldn't remember seeing in all her twelve years. She allowed herself to wrap her arms around them both.

Tommy ran back to them, his little shoes tapping on the worn wooden floor. 'Did they hear me, Mary?' he shouted. 'Did they?' He'd been told the news too, in his own way. She swooped him into her arms and nodded. 'Everyone can hear you!' she replied. 'All the way to Whitechapel and back!' He clapped his hands.

They moved to the table for supper, sharing a meal of thick slices of bread and the promise of meat for Sunday. 'Mr Turner must truly be heaven sent,' Anne said, lifting her head in thanks. 'I wonder at your sour face, Mary. You aren't fretting over foolish things, I hope?'

'Not fretting,' Mary said, pushing a crumb around her plate. 'I just wonder how he's changed so.'

Anne took a sharp breath. 'By grace! Or by having his heart opened!' Charles put his hand on Mary's. 'We couldn't have asked for a better friend,' he said.

Mary met his eyes and nodded. Their trust in the man seemed like fine glass; she feared one crack might shatter it. She could tell they thought of all the ways this meant a better life – no more cold mornings by the stove, scraping for bits of fuel; no more winter coughs that never went away.

Tommy chattered on about having cake, and Mary laughed again at his silly little mouth. Their voices grew full, alive in their once-silent rooms, carrying on far into the evening. Each day after brought new smiles, new songs hummed under Anne's breath. She straightened their two rooms, making space for things they would now have. Charles walked tall and proud. He held Mary close and told her again and again of how fine life would be. He left each morning before dawn and came back each night to warm smiles and warm food.

'I don't like that Mr Turner,' she whispered to Tommy one night before bed.

'He's too sweet. Like sugar that melts away.' Tommy wiggled, half understanding, mostly not.

Anne had overheard. 'Mary! I don't want to hear another word against him. Mr Turner has been as good as gold to us. Isn't that right, Charles?' He nodded, though quieter than before.

'We owe him much,' he said, 'and you, little lady, owe him your school and all those books you want.' Mary hugged Tommy close and saw her words upset her parents. They ate until their bellies were full, Tommy rubbing his as if it were a magic lamp.

Before long, Charles came home with a strange look. Mary saw his eyes shift away.

'What is it?' Anne asked.

He sat down slowly.

'Charles? You're pale,' Anne went on, worried and tugging at his sleeve.

'Things aren't quite right at the docks,' he said at last. 'It's just... there's talk.'

Mary saw Anne hold herself in. 'But you've just done your work. Whatever's happening has nothing to do with you, right?'

'We'll see. I'm sure it will be fine.'

Mary sat silent, hearing everything.

Charles could not stop pacing the room. 'I'll take a walk,' he said, trying to be like himself again. 'Just down the street. I'll see who I can find. Maybe go see if Wilson's in.'

Anne gave him a quick smile. 'Go on, then,' she said, trying to believe it was nothing at all.

The house was silent.

Anne sat still, her hands folded too tightly in her lap. Her eyes never left the door.

Mary had tried to put Tommy to bed, but he wouldn't stop asking.

Where's Da? When is he coming back?

She had no answers. No lies would come to her lips.

Anne had barely spoken since it happened. When Mary knelt beside her, she could see the fine tremor in her mother's fingers, the way her lips moved without sound, prayers or curses she couldn't say aloud.

Mary swallowed the lump in her throat.

'Turner?' Anne finally spoke. She was sitting on the floor. Her eyes were glassy, far away, no hope in them now.

Mary said nothing, though the look on her face spoke more than any words. Her mouth set hard, lips a thin line. 'He'll pay for it,' Mary finally said. 'He will.'

# CHAPTER 4

The family hardly slept. Charles's night out was a night away, a night and a day and another night. Anne was wasted by then, a husk of herself, always looking through the door. She'd get up suddenly, out of her chair, and Mary would pull her back down.

On the second day, a knock rattled their bones. A boy, about her age, shoved a dirty envelope at Mary, barely meeting her eyes. 'Said I might get a penny for it,' he said. 'Go on, then. Be kind, Miss.' She threw him one as she tore the letter open.

Anne took it. 'They'll make him a trial. He'll be back.' She took Mary by the arms, looking at her. 'He'll be back!' Her mother's eyes made Mary believe it.

Tommy stayed at Mrs Wilson's, left there to forget. But Mary couldn't forget. Even when she tried. Not even when her mother said the court would let Charles go. It wouldn't. The trial happened fast, faster than Mary's heart. The lawyers, the judge, the other men. They all said the same word. Guilty. Mary could hardly hear it.

Anne did, though. She screamed and pulled at her hair, pulled at Mary's shoulder as she fell against her, weeping, bones and breath and prayers. But Mary didn't cry. She held her mother tight.

Anne broke in the days that followed. Her voice went gone, leaving a shell of sounds in their small rooms. Mary gave up on everything but caring for her. The family stayed inside, curtains drawn tight, missing Charles but fearing what would happen when he returned. Not knowing what would happen when he didn't. Mary missed Tommy, but kept him far away. They couldn't let him see. Not yet. Not until things changed.

Mrs Wilson came often at first, a blur of worried words and other peoples' stories. 'They had no proof,' she said, again and again. 'Nothing at all!' Mary listened, feeling nothing. She didn't need proof; she didn't need more than she already knew.

'Turner,' she said one night. Just the name. But it made Anne sit up.

'Yes.'

They were left on their own when the last letter came. It fell through the mail slot, landing like a dead bird at the door. 'When, Mary?' Anne asked, not even reading it, not even able to touch it. 'When?'

'Tomorrow. We have to go.'

She got out of her chair and pushed Mary with her, daring herself to move, to do what she thought she could. They went back to the cold street, knowing it would be the last time. The walk was short but felt long. As long as the years it would be without him.

'Charles!' Anne screamed as they reached the gates. A constable shook his head. 'Charles, my love!' she screamed again. But he couldn't hear. Or wouldn't.

Anne gasped and crumpled to the ground. She didn't rise. She didn't move at all. Mary pulled her mother away, not looking back. Not needing to look back.

By the time Mary got them home, Anne was just breath, a shadow of the person she had been. 'Gone,' she said, and it was more than a word. 'He won't be back.' Mary put her to bed, covered her with love and all the warmth she could give.

When they received word at last, the final one, it was Mary alone. Her mother spared her the pain, leaving her asleep as if that would be enough. Mary heard Tommy in the hallway, calling, singing, waiting for his sister to come. She heard him louder than she heard anything else, and it gave her hope. She pressed herself into him, alive and full of something good.

'Tommy!' she cried, lifting him high. 'Back soon!' he shouted, giggling and sure of it. He never knew he'd been gone, never knew what he'd been saved from.

'Never leave us,' she said, more to herself than to him.

He smiled wide, and his cheeks pinked. 'Never, Mary!'

'That's right. We'll stay. We'll stay together.' She pulled him close and thought of Anne, thought of Charles, thought of what they'd lost, and how much she still had.

The days dragged on. Mrs Wilson and her lot stopped coming. The only noise in the house was the click of the mail slot when it rattled and banged.

The very last of the letters said what she knew already, what Anne couldn't bear to say.

'Dead by the hang.'

Anne tucked it under the mattress, as if hiding it would make it untrue. Then she curled around her children, holding them as if she could keep them from vanishing too.

'We'll be alright.'

'Are you?' Tommy asked.

She hugged him until she was. She said nothing for a long while, then whispered so quietly she barely knew she'd said it.

'Yes.'

# CHAPTER 5

$\mathcal{T}$he memory of Charles still clung to the docks when they bundled Anne, Mary, and Tommy out of the house. They left Cripplegate, where they had ended the journey in shame and darkness. Mary helped her mother carry the faded valise, the sole survivor of their belongings. Three weeks unpaid, and they were as good as dead for their landlord. Mary asked where they were going, but Anne couldn't lift her head to answer, and so they trudged through the cold night. At last, they arrived at a creaking door in a pitiful street of Whitechapel and found the filthiest corner room available.

The tenement was overflowing with broken families and lost souls. Mary coughed at the stench as they crossed the hallway, Tommy clutching her skirt, eyes wide with the thrill of seeing such squalor for the first time. The landlady motioned them up the stairs, holding Tommy for a moment by his collar as Anne climbed.

'Hardly worth taking,' she said, nodding to his rail-thin legs.

They settled into a space that held no more than a straw

mattress and a rusted stove. Water ran in rivulets down the walls, and rats outnumbered the cockroaches.

'It's only temporary,' their mother assured them. 'Just until I find work.' But work was scarce for a woman with the taint of a criminal's widow, and what little money they had would dwindle rapidly.

She sat heavily on the mattress, pulled Mary close, and then cried as if they had buried Charles in her arms. Mary rested her head on Anne's shoulder and felt the bones of it beneath the skin. Tommy watched them, eyes too wide for a four-year-old.

'Is Da with the angels, Ma?'

Mary squeezed his hand and said he was.

Weeks passed, and the cold that had greeted them the first night seeped into their skin. Anne coughed constantly, but she managed to pull herself up and make small improvements in their room, each day brightening the space with some meager item salvaged from the streets. A chipped plate became their centrepiece.

Mary and Tommy spent afternoons watching the fishmongers' stalls in the hopes of a scrap, running home with shrivelled turnips or a bruised apple. The nights dragged on, and Anne grew quieter and weaker. On the fourth Sunday, she did not rise from bed.

Mary knew.

'Ma, you're cold,' said Tommy, when they returned with half a loaf under Mary's coat. 'You should get warm, like me.' He climbed into her lap. Anne's smile was distant. Mary put the loaf next to her, but Anne didn't touch it.

'You two eat it. You'll need it more.' Mary shook her head, and her hair brushed the flour from Tommy's cheeks.

'Eat something, Ma. Please.'

But Anne's voice was far away, and her breaths were

shorter each time. Her eyes fluttered open. 'Charles?' she murmured. 'Is that you?'

'No, Mother, it's Mary,' she said, pressing a hand to her forehead. It burned beneath her touch.

'My Mary. You'll take care of him, won't you? I know you will. I'm so proud of my Mary.' Her hands found her daughter's for a moment. She coughed, then slipped into a stillness that filled the room. It was more than Mary's heart could bear.

They wandered the streets for hours while Anne's body lay stiff and alone. They could not stay. The tenement women peered out from behind their doorways, afraid to take them in, afraid to turn them away. Mary covered Tommy with an old curtain that night, his head resting on her lap, her legs too numb to feel him.

They awoke on the doorstep. The landlady sneered, crossed herself, and muttered 'Catholics' under her breath before letting them back in. Mary filled a basin with cold water and scrubbed Tommy from head to toe. They were clean enough to be pitied, and a few small coins appeared on their window ledge.

Tommy asked when Ma was coming back, and Mary had to remind him, though she could hardly speak. Her voice felt like gravel.

'In heaven with Da. But we're here, Tommy. You and me, together.'

She held him tight as he squirmed away and watched the landlady kick at something on the doorstep. A shoeless man clutched a newspaper to his chest. It was an eviction notice.

'Ma never got that sick. I think she just misses Da.'

Mary swallowed, knowing that part of him was right. 'Heaven,' she said. 'That's why. They wanted her there.'

# CHAPTER 6

ary cleaned their corner with vinegar scraps and newsprint, borrowed needle and thread, and sewed a rough bed of rags for Tommy. He settled down on it, laughing at the spring of it beneath him.

Anne had hidden a few coins under the mattress, so Mary stretched them as far as they would go. Each morning, they walked to the baker's for day-old buns, and she asked after the landlady's children for pennies and stew bones. At night, Tommy ran about the tenement, wild and laughing. 'We're all orphans,' he shouted at the men who drank in the stairwell. One raised his bottle, but Mary grabbed him before he could say more.

They heard the first coughs two days later. The room grew colder. Mary brought Tommy into her arms to warm him. She shared stories about what their life would be like once she could afford new shoes. He wanted the story of the horse.

'You've heard it, Tommy. Ten times, at least.'

'I want it again.'

She took a little carved figure from her pocket. The

horse's paint had long worn away, but Tommy's eyes were wide as the first day.

'Daddy made it for me when I was just your age,' she said. 'I didn't think I'd let it go. But it's yours, Tommy. You'll take care of it.'

He ran his fingers over its face and kicked his feet with delight.

'Be careful. You'll wake them all.' But Mary was laughing now too, despite herself. She pulled him close and refused to let go.

Days became weeks. The horse's legs broke and were mended, its coat rubbed to the dull shine of old wax. The basin filled with water again, and Mary made Tommy soak in it until he cried. She went from shop to shop looking for anything they could eat, any bit of work that wouldn't see them starved. The baker had hired a girl younger than she, and the fishmonger would only trade in secret, old bread for half a crab.

Mary brought it all home, fed Tommy first, and prayed that it would last. When it didn't, she pawned the little horse and used the coin to buy him some cheese. He ate slowly and slept more each day. At night, the whiskey bottles rolled in the stairwell, but Mary held him until he was asleep.

They went to their landlady's door. She held him in her arms, knocked, and promised to pay.

'We're not a charity.'

'But we're desperate,' Mary said, feeling his warmth against her chest, knowing that was the last of it.

Tommy called to the little horse. Mary's hands were shaking. The woman snorted and closed the door.

When Tommy wouldn't eat, she gathered all her courage and made her way back to Cripplegate. The siblings arrived at Cripplegate Workhouse. The children on the street called it Turner's Workhouse. Mary turned her face so no one would know. Tommy lay limp in her arms.

The gate swung open – the guard barked, 'Clear off!' as he nearly tripped over her. She was too exhausted to move.

'Please. I must speak to Mr Turner.'

Turner appeared at the gate, his eyes narrowing when he saw her.

'Please, sir,' she begged. 'Tommy's sick. So sick. We have no one else.'

'And why would I help Charles Bennett's brats?'

'Please, sir. I can work. You know I will.'

'Work?' He stepped back. 'Get the fever out of him first. Can't have it infecting everyone here.'

Mary clutched Tommy tighter, refusing to let him go, but he took a step back, careful to avoid touching her.

'He's dying,' she said, knowing the words had no effect.

'Plenty of children die in this city. One more won't make a difference.'

The gate slammed shut and they went back to the tenement. Mary's head spun, and her eyes were too dry to cry. Mary took the rest of the money Anne had left and gave it to the landlady.

'Not enough,' she said, pocketing the coins anyway.

'Please, I can work, I'll do anything.'

'You can stay one more night. But I need you out tomorrow.'

Mary lay beside Tommy, knowing what was coming. She could almost hear it breathing in the room, a whisper of smoke and dust that would not go away. Her heart burned, and she did not close her eyes.

She spooned bits of food into Tommy's mouth, and he looked better for an hour, maybe two. They wrapped themselves in the curtain that covered the door, and she told him the story of the horse again, even without it there. Tommy laughed and coughed and rolled in his bed, but the fever burned him hotter each time. She watched him melt away, his face growing dimmer in the early hours, his breath shorter and farther apart. His eyes closed, and he was still.

'It's all right,' Mary said, tears streaming down her face. 'You can go to Mam and Da. They're waiting for you.'

Mary clutched him to her chest and felt the smallness of him. Just a child. Just a boy. His little soul had abandoned his body.

The landlady threw open the door, but Mary refused to let him go.

The parish buried Tommy in Cripplegate Cemetery alongside others who had died that week. They had given him nothing but a pauper's stone, his name carved into it like a cut in her heart.

Mary stood by her now-buried brother long after the brief service had concluded, ignoring the parish officer's impatient shifting beside her.

'Time to go, girl,' he said finally. 'Can't stay here all day.'

'Where am I to go?'

The officer sighed. 'Workhouse is the only place for you now. Unless you've got family willing to take you in?'

Mary shook her head, unable to comprehend that she was now completely alone in the world.

'Workhouse it is, then,' the officer said, not unkindly. 'Come along.'

Mary knelt by the grave, pressing her hand to the damp earth. 'I'm sorry, Tommy,' she whispered. 'I couldn't save you. I wish I could have done more.'

# CHAPTER 7

*C*ripplegate Workhouse loomed ahead. The high walls of Turner's prison, hunched like an animal ready to spring. Its windows stared black and empty on the deserted street, and only the frost glistened on the pavements. Clinging to the sleeves of a passing day, a thin fog wrapped Mary's feet and shadowed the bundle that was her belongings. She swallowed against the thing lodged in her throat, threatening to choke her with each step. The click of the gate lock seemed to startle the ghosts in the courtyard. As Mary passed through the gates, the smell hit her first – boiled cabbage, and something else, something that reminded her of defeat. She thought she'd definitely miss her mum's porridge.

'This way,' the officer said, steering her towards a door marked 'Admissions'.

The matron was a thin woman with lips pressed into a permanent line of disapproval. 'Name?' she barked at her desk.

Mary straightened her shoulders, lifting her chin in a gesture that would have made her father proud.

'Mary Bennett,' she said clearly, holding on to the name like it was all she had left. 'My name is Mary Bennett.'

The matron kept taking Mary's details in a bored voice, asking questions that scraped against Mary's raw grief.

'Parents?'

'Dead.'

'Siblings?'

'Gone.'

The matron barely looked up from her writing.

'Any other relatives?'

'No.'

The scratching of the pen continued, indifferent. Finally, she snapped the ledger shut. 'Wait here. The master will want to see you.'

Mary stood in the cold corridor outside the admissions office, her threadbare shawl pulled tight around her shoulders, waiting for the last person she wanted to see – and she hated she had no choice.

When the door to Turner's office opened, Mary forced her spine straight. Turner stood in the doorway, blocking the light spilling from his office.

'Mary Bennett, I didn't expect to see you here again. I thought I made myself clear when you came begging.'

'Tommy's dead.' It was the first time she had said the words aloud. They ripped her chest open. 'I've nowhere else to go.'

Turner gestured toward the hallway. 'Infirmary's down there. Doctor needs to check you first. Can't have scarlatina spreading through my workhouse.'

The doctor's examination was perfunctory – a quick look at her throat, a hand on her forehead, questions about symptoms she might be hiding. Mary answered in monosyllables, her mind elsewhere. When he pronounced her free of contagion, Turner nodded curtly.

The matron handed the ledger to Turner and Mary followed him to his office. Somewhere deep in the building, a hollow clanging and shouting vibrated like a drum against her ears. His office was warm with a roaring fire that spit cinders and smoke into the air. He gestured at her to wait by the door, then sat at his desk and pretended to sort papers, ignoring her presence. She glanced around at the heavy curtains. They would have kept Anne and Tommy warm in their last days, she thought.

When his voice came again, it sliced through the silence like a blade. 'Hope you don't think you're getting special treatment.'

Mary flinched, biting her lip to keep the tears from spilling over. 'No.'

'Or that I'll pay any attention to whining.'

'I won't cause any trouble, I promise.'

'Better not.' He looked up, piercing her with cold eyes. 'Ten, aren't you?'

'Twelve.'

'Excellent. Capable of work then.'

She nodded.

Turner waved a hand in dismissal. 'The matron will take you to the girl's dormitory.'

As Mary followed her out, Turner called after her. 'Remember, girl – you're here on my charity now. I expect gratitude and obedience.'

Mary didn't turn back. She knew what Turner saw when he looked at her – not a child who had lost everything, but another body to work, another number in his business, another mouth that would bring him parish funds.

The matron led her into the labyrinth of the workhouse, through dim passages and narrow stairwells, past rooms teeming with pale faces and too-thin bodies. In the girl's dormitory, rows of beds stretched away into the gloom, a single candle flickering as if struggling to light the space. A hunched woman came forward.

'Another one for you,' the matron said, as if Mary was a parcel being delivered.

'Come on then,' the woman mumbled. Her hand was dry and cold as bone as it pulled Mary away.

'I'm starving. When can I eat?' The door swung shut on the matron's answer: the faint sound of a laugh.

The dormitory was an echo of Mary's past fears. She saw herself mirrored in every face. One moment they appeared large and menacing, the next, shrunk to almost nothing under threadbare blankets. Some coughed. Others lay still as corpses. A few gathered at the foot of their bunks, whispering and darting their eyes towards the newcomer.

They made their way down a row of narrow beds. Thin mattresses sagged on iron frames. It was hard to tell if they were worse than what Mary remembered at the tenement; then, at least, there had been Tommy to hold close. Now, everything seemed vast and empty. The woman stopped, pointing to a bunk.

'Yours. I don't want to hear any complaints.' The voice faded as she moved away, as dry as her hands and almost as harsh.

Mary stood still for a moment, clutching the bundle of her belongings to her chest. She had only to let go for them to unroll, revealing nothing but one patched dress and a photograph that had already started to fade, and that Mary feared would become the memory of a memory. There was her mother, holding Tommy's hand, smiling as if they still had everything ahead of them.

She sank onto the mattress, finally allowing herself to

remember. The fever had come so fast. Their tiny room was no match for its chill and damp. Turner slamming the door, saying they didn't want infection, didn't care where they went, as long as they left. How many other doors had they tried, she wondered, before her mother gave up and took Tommy to the streets of Whitechapel? The picture stared up at her from the bed, and she felt it accusing her of what she already knew: You should have done more.

More coughing, more whispers. Footsteps on the stairs, a girl chasing a mouse across the floor. The daily chaos of workhouse life continued its steady rhythm.

Mary got up slowly, clutching a borrowed blanket to ward off the draught. On the far side of the room, a window gaped where a pane was missing, and it was through this that she escaped, unseen.

A deep longing brought her to Tommy's grave in a quiet corner of the cemetery just behind her new home. Mary stood, and the blanket's weight pulled at her, made her hunch and curl, until it was like a smaller version of the workhouse itself.

'I'm sorry. But I promise, Tommy, I'll become a nurse. I won't let what happened to you happen to others. I swear it.'

Her voice dissolved into a sob, and she wrapped her arms around her knees, a lonely bundle against the dirt.

A few minutes later, Mary's head snapped up, and she saw a boy around her age, hair as dark as her brother's and a face like hers. Orphaned.

'Didn't mean to scare you. Sneaking out on your first day? Impressive.'

He flopped down beside her. 'I'm Samuel Brown. Though I like Sam better.'

'Mary.'

'I know,' he nodded easily, as if they'd always known each other. 'Master thought you'd bring scarlet fever in. He thinks the world's in here to kill him, and he's probably right.'

Mary shifted her gaze from the stone to his face. She couldn't help but laughing. 'You shouldn't be here, Sam. What if they catch you?'

'It's probably the least of my worries. But anyway, they don't check until supper.'

He rubbed his thumb over the letters on Tommy's stone. 'Was that someone you knew?'

'My little brother.'

'I am really sorry, Mary.'

Seconds turned into minutes until Sam came closer, studying her face. 'You're different compared to the other children.'

'Different how?'

'You've still got fight in your eyes.'

Mary looked away. 'Maybe I just haven't been here long enough.'

'How'd you end up here, then?'

'My family died,' Mary said, the words coming out harshly. 'My father paid for something he didn't do. Then my mother couldn't bear it and got sick out of desperation. Then Tommy got scarlet fever and...' She couldn't finish.

Sam nodded, understanding in his eyes. 'My mam died in childbirth. Me dad in a factory accident.'

'It's so sad you never got to know your mum. When did your dad die?'

'I've been here three years now.'

'Three years?' Mary couldn't keep the horror from her voice. 'How do you stand it?'

Sam watched her. He saw her as he would a map, tracing each river and mountain of loss until he knew the way to navigate. Then he spoke, his words alive with the thing she had almost forgotten. Hope.

'You find ways. There's a gap in the fence behind the coal shed. Sometimes I slip out, just for an hour or two. See the sky without bars across it.'

'Will you take me with you?'

Sam nodded. 'And you know what I say? Let's show Turner we're more than mouths to feed.' He laughed, and Mary's heart lifted at the sound.

Sam's shoulder touched Mary's. Then, softly, he asked, 'What happened to your father? You told me he paid for something he didn't do.'

Mary's fingers curled into her skirt. She knew this question would come eventually. She glanced at Sam – he wasn't pushing, just waiting. She exhaled. 'Turner set him up. Framed him for stealing at the docks. He had him hanged for it.'

Sam stiffened beside her. 'Hanged?'

She nodded. 'Couldn't even say goodbye.'

Sam's hands clenched into fists against his knees. His usual easygoing manner was gone. 'That bastard. He plays at being a good man, but he's filth. The worst kind.'

'And I promise that someday I'll tell the world about men like Turner. I'll make sure everyone knows what he did to your family.'

Mary looked at him, this boy she barely knew who somehow understood her pain, her anger, her need for justice.

'We'll survive this place,' Sam said, taking her hand. 'We'll get out. We'll become what we want to be.'

The cemetery fell into silence around them, settling like snow. Two children have made their vows, said their dreams aloud.

A distant bell rang somewhere in the building.

'Supper,' Sam said, standing up. 'Hurry, we need to go back. If you're late, you don't eat.'

34

# CHAPTER 8

*M*ary lay on her side in the row of beds nearest the wall. The bell rang. Her breath clouded the cold air in puffs. It mingled with the moans of waking children. The pit-pat of bare feet across the stones. There were days, not long past, when she had dreaded the tolling of that bell. But lately it had become an odd comfort – each clang marked another hour that Sam was there with her, facing the worst together. It made her feel less alone. The door to the dormitory opened, admitting the black-booted figure of John Turner. He barked his orders, mouth twisting, eyes pinched with hatred of weakness and sloth and dirt and everything that Mary was learning to despise as much as he did.

Dragging herself from her bed, Mary joined the slow shuffle towards the washing line. Her body felt the bruise of the past day. The soreness of scrubbing boards and lifting coal and stitching endless, fraying linens. Behind her, girls fumbled and cried softly, made stupid with hunger and chill. The youngest, barely six, fought back her tears. Mary gave the girl a small piece of bread saved from last night's supper and felt, for a moment, a sliver of lightness in her heart.

'Mary! There you are.' Sam's voice brought colour into the drab world.

As they went about the day's first task, Sam held himself with a defiance that Mary admired and tried to match. He never flinched from Turner's orders, though Mary's hands ached at the sight of the blisters on his fingers.

Their morning passed in fits and bursts. As long as they kept the pace, they stole moments for themselves. Exchanging a grin over mounds of grey, sudsy water. Helping each other lift the heavier baskets of coal. Mary didn't feel the exhaustion when Sam was there. His presence turned the harsh clang of the bells into a metronome, beating their shared rhythm.

By afternoon, they were sent to the yard. Chores stretched endlessly. The softening of bones and limbs into a muted pain. Turner kept watch like a crow on a dying branch. Mary and Sam fell into line, moving with the others like clockwork toys – brittle but running. They gathered behind the wash-house, sharing the meal no larger than a poor man's penny, murmuring through mouthfuls.

'I've an extra bit of bread today,' Sam said. 'Trade you for half your gruel.'

Mary nodded, stifling a laugh. 'Is it a new recipe? Double rat tail?'

'Better. Triple!'

They took turns, scraping the bowl until nothing but a thin rim of watery grey remained. In such things, they made a game of it. Mary remembered her father's teasing way at supper, before everything had turned and broken and led her here. The sudden sweep of grief took her voice away.

Sam touched her hand. 'You're thinking of them, aren't you?'

Mary nodded. The silence between them was not awkward or forced. It carried memories, and that was enough. But she could feel the words pressing at her chest, wanting release.

'I used to think it would get easier. Being alone,' she said at last.

'Not alone now.' Sam's grip was gentle and firm.

The bell sounded again, a strident call. Time for the next round of work. Time for their bones to feel the break again. Mary watched as Sam rubbed his fingers on his ragged trousers, adjusting to the strain. He caught her look and straightened.

'Come on, Mary. I've an idea.' His whisper was full of mischief.

They returned the empty bowl and snuck out, breathing quick in case the crow spotted them and brought his vengeance down. Past the low fence, where weeds grew defiant in the snow-speckled mud. Through the gap behind the coal shed. Into the world beyond the high walls. Mary felt the tingle of excitement under her skin.

There, on the other side, they laughed for the joy of being young and outside and free. The street stretched wide and silent. Though the chill of early evening was hard, it was not the stale breath of the Workhouse. Mary tilted her face to the sky, imagining stars. They sat on the kerb, revelling in the open air, a pair of shivering birds. Mary knew they must return soon, before the bell. Before the black boots and the cracked leather belt came hunting. But for now, she let herself float on that fragile cloud of freedom.

'Sam, thank you.'

He gave her a lopsided grin. 'We make a habit of it, yeah?'

And they had, in those stolen moments between the grind of work and the call of bells. In the endless cycle of days that Mary thought might break her spirit but only forged it harder. She liked to think her brother would be proud, wherever he was. Wherever her mother and father had gone to wait.

They walked back through the gap. Into the stale breath of the Workhouse.

And Turner was there.

His face was stone, chiselled with purpose. 'The Master is not so blind as some would think.' Mary's chest tightened. The other girls shrank from his presence, stepping quick and wide of him as he advanced. He stopped before Mary and Sam. For one glimmering second, she thought his expression softened – but no, she must have imagined it. He bore down on them.

'You've found a way out. It will not help you now.'

They were at attention, backs ramrod straight, but Turner's eyes remained on Mary. 'Miss Bennett. I fear this place has proved a bad influence on your moral character. For a girl of your age, a position in domestic service may be what you need. Yes, I think so. It is settled. I shall see to it myself.'

Mary felt Sam shift beside her, saw his fists clench and release and clench again.

'Sir...'

'Be quiet, boy. You have a lot to answer for. I am no longer blind to your tricks.'

Mary dared a glance at Sam. It made her heart stop in her chest and set the entire world spinning. 'I'll be all right.'

'This very evening,' Turner continued, loud enough for all the dormitories to hear. 'By tomorrow you'll be earning your keep at Branscombe's.' He gave a sour laugh. 'And far from this nonsense.' He did not need to say it – the threat was plain. The fear and the warning. You will be gone. You will be alone.

Sam met her eyes. He had the expression of a drowning

man, arms lashed by a tide that he could not hope to swim against. The bell clanged, a single note that sounded in Mary's bones like the sharp toll of yet another funeral.

# CHAPTER 9

*T*he grand house rose from the ground like a cliff, with high iron railings and rows of windows. Mary stood with her small, battered case and watched as the cart disappeared from view. Gone was the man who had delivered her. Gone the shouts and din of the crowded East End. It had taken two hours and another lifetime to reach Branscombe's.

She was not meant to stand there idling. The letter in her pocket, signed with John Turner's impatient scrawl, made that plain. Lady Branscombe expected her at precisely five o'clock. The great door opened. Mary snapped to attention. A broad-shouldered man beckoned her inside, wasting no time on words. His movements were quick, sure as they stripped her of coat and bonnet and scarf and things that had offered a measure of comfort in the chill.

Inside, everything was colour and grandeur. Stiff-backed chairs, carved with flowers. Velvet curtains. Ornaments of blue and white china on the tables. Mary felt a creature made of dirt and rags.

The man said nothing, moved in silence through the

house as she followed. Her eyes stung. At last, they came to a narrow staircase and descended. Voices came from below. And there, in the dim light of the lower corridor, a scene of some confusion. A young girl, not much older than herself, fought tears as a stern while an elderly woman barked instructions. 'She will be back with Turner, if she cannot do better!'

Mary felt her heart quicken. She was not the first to come from the workhouse.

The old woman, the housekeeper, was dressed in a plain brown frock, less fine than Mary's imagination had pictured. Her expression was hawk-like, her small eyes sharp beneath a severe crown of white hair. 'Mary Bennett?'

Mary's mouth was dry as sawdust. 'Yes, miss.'

'Mrs Goode will do. Well, what are you waiting for, then? There's much to do. Follow, follow, follow!'

Mrs Goode set a pace that left no room for idleness. The halls were endless. They passed more rooms than Mary could count. They passed more fine things than she had ever seen. They passed other servants – maids in black and white and long lace aprons. Each one moved quick and silent, looking neither right nor left. Mary took it all in with wide eyes. She wanted to scream her fear. Her aloneness.

They arrived at the kitchens. She hardly remembered the way.

There was a single, narrow window. It smelled of onions and soapy water and something faintly sweet. Brown paper parcels covered the long table, an army of stiffened hats. Mary reached to open one.

'Never mind that,' Mrs Goode snapped. 'Laundry first. There's a good half-day of washing and then some. See that tub there? Fill it. Water's up the stairs. You have legs, haven't you? Use them, then!'

It took only a moment for Mary to remember her way of

it. The creak and shift of unsteady buckets in her small hands. Water from the long, clean sink at the top of the stairs. Her thoughts turned to the gap in the Workhouse fence, the freedom of the open street. Sam's warm touch on a cold morning. She set her jaw and swallowed the ache. Mary was not used to leaving a job undone. Even that first day, despite her confusion, she found a way to bear it.

Mary didn't know how many hours had passed when she heard footsteps and an unfamiliar voice. Soft. Gentle as the stroke of feathers.

'Mrs Goode said you were the new girl.'

Mary turned. The figure in the door was tall and thin. Almost as thin as herself. A lady, if her dress and voice and carriage were to be believed.

'I am. Miss.'

The lady in the door smiled. Not with her mouth, which was a pale, thin line. But her eyes were warm. Friendly. Mary found herself trusting them. Trusting her.

'You're young. But I think you'll be all right. I'm Rosamund, but you can call me Rosa.' She paused briefly and glanced toward the stairs, as if ensuring they were alone. 'That is quite a load you've been given. May I help you?'

'I've done worse.' She did not mean to say it as a boast. She said it because it was true.

'Brave girl. We need more of them, we do.'

'Are you...' Mary didn't know what she was allowed to ask. 'Are you the governess?'

Rosamund gave a half-laugh, barely a breath of air. 'When Lady Branscombe keeps me.' Another pause. 'I used to be a nurse.'

Mary's eyes widened, suddenly bright. 'A nurse? My brother. He was sick and... I wish I could've known what to do. I always wanted to be...' She stopped, suddenly fearful she'd said too much.

Rosamund studied her for a moment, thoughtful. 'I see.' She reached into her pocket, withdrew a small scrap of folded paper, scribbled something quickly on it, then placed it discreetly into Mary's hand.

'Take this,' she whispered. 'And keep it hidden. If you want, perhaps I can teach you a few things, quietly. Mind.'

Mary's heart quickened. She slipped the note quickly into her sleeve. 'Yes. Please, Rosa.'

Rosamund smiled again. 'Let me know if you need anything, Mary.'

She was gone, but something new lingered in the small room. The smell of soapy water. Onions. And, once again, hope.

When Mary finished the laundry, it was dark. She slept on a pallet by the scullery door, away from the other maids. She dreamed of Sam. She dreamed she was a nurse, making her family proud. In the morning, she returned to her work. Water. Stairs. More washing. Stiff, brown paper parcels. Mary found time to open the note. It was filled with numbers and strange words. They swam before her eyes. Rosamund passed by as Mary puzzled over the paper, carrying linens up the stairs.

'Medical terms,' she said softly. The blue and white ornaments rattled faintly. 'Let me know if you need anything.'

The days settled into weeks. Mary's hands ached with the old, familiar soreness. She scrubbed and scoured, washed and carried, filled and emptied and filled again. The uncertainty of her arrival was now replaced by the dulling edge of fatigue. She saw no more of Lady Branscombe than the swoop of fine skirts across the distant end of a long hallway. But Mrs Goode was watchful, relentless. The work was no less punishing than the Workhouse, though Mary felt less the dirt of it and more the loneliness. When Rosamund passed and found Mary alone, she sometimes stayed to offer a small lesson, a brief smile, a paper filled with the words that Mary loved.

She did not forget Sam. She could not forget. At night, she traced his name in her mind, like her finger on the pages of Rosamund's notes. She was certain it had been him, whispering soft and low, in the dark of a half-dream. A trick of the cold, she thought. A wish for the warmth of his company. 'Not alone now,' she thought he said.

'Not alone now,' Mary repeated, hearing the familiar music of it. Then she closed her eyes, turned her cheek to the side, and hoped.

# CHAPTER 10

While the Branscombe household breathed in sleep, the stillness settled like a heavy eiderdown. Mary crept past Mrs Goode's snores, holding her breath at every creak of the boards beneath her shoes. Rosamund opened her door a mere inch, a quick smile passing her lips as Mary slipped inside and perched on the edge of the narrow bed. They whispered under the sputtering lamplight until Mary knew the papers Rosamund had scribbled on by heart. The names of body parts and medicinal plants unspooled in her mind with miraculous clarity. In those moments, the fire of understanding burned bright within her, unlike anything she had known.

Rosamund watched her with pride. 'This,' Mary said to the curled edge of a page, 'is the clavicle. And here... belladinna. That's for when the patient is hurting, right?'

'Belladonna, Mary. Belladonna. For spasms and pain. Remember that.'

Mary nodded eagerly, repeating the words under her breath. Her heart thumped with each new term, each new connection that formed in her head like stars finding their constellation in a dark sky. The thin sheets of paper were filled with more information than she could ever dream of, yet she felt herself absorbing every line, every letter.

Rosamund reached for a new slip. 'You've a gift, Mary. I've not seen such determination.'

A rare smile broke over Mary's lips. She had lived with shadows too long to mistake this for anything other than light. Would they be proud of me?

Her parents. And Tommy – dear, sweet Tommy – who would have laughed and said she was too clever by half. I wish you could see me now. She swallowed the thought.

Outside the window, the first fingers of dawn tugged at the night, pulling it apart seam by seam. Mary rose reluctantly, tucking the precious papers into her apron, and stole back down the dim hallways. Her own bed, when she slipped into it, was cold and barely slept in.

The morning routine was a march of familiar footsteps and complaints. In the kitchen, the scullery hissed and steamed like some great factory machine, and the kitchen maid – an ill-tempered girl with arms like windmill sails – complained about her share of the work.

'Look at you,' she said, her mouth pinched and sour. 'Always ten steps ahead. The rest of us can't catch our breath.'

Mary said nothing. She scrubbed and rinsed and polished until her hands were raw, doing her best to look like a servant who thought of nothing but her duty. As she left the kitchen with a tray for the upstairs rooms, she could feel the maid's grumbles like the gnats of East End summer – biting, persistent, but easily swatted aside.

Upstairs, Mrs Goode was an ever-watchful figure. 'There's too much whispering among the girls these days,' she said, glancing at Mary in the hall. 'I won't have it.'

Mary nodded, dropping her eyes to the floor. She had learned how to move quietly around Mrs Goode's authority, like water finding its way around a rock. The old house-keeper was strict, yes, but not unkind; she scolded loudly, but never struck. Mary thought that her bark was worse than her bite.

That morning, Mary made extra work for herself in the library, the one room Mrs Goode seldom bothered to check. The air was thick with the smell of polished wood and ink, a world apart from the scorched haze of London's streets. Mary dusted the high shelves, letting her fingers run over the spines of the books, a longing unfurling inside her that she could not quite contain.

The door opened, and Mary froze in place, certain she had been found out. But it was not Mrs Goode who entered. It was a young woman Mary had only seen from a distance. Lilly Branscombe. She was fair and quick, moving across the room with a liveliness that Mary thought seemed out of place in this still and quiet house.

'Are you the new maid?' Lilly asked, stopping to observe Mary with an interest that was unexpected.

Mary hesitated, unsure if she should speak or simply duck her head. 'Yes, Miss.'

Lilly sat on the edge of a large desk, her dress pooling around her like some great bright petal. She tilted her head, the beginnings of a smile on her lips. 'I've seen you, you know. You move as if the house is haunted.'

Mary flushed, unsure how to reply. 'I try not to disturb anyone, Miss.'

'Call me Lilly. And you've already disturbed me – by dusting my favourite books.'

Mary bit her lip, torn between the fear of being caught at something she should not be doing and the strange, new sensation that she was being invited to stay. She set down her cloth, watching Lilly's every move.

'Can you read them?' Lilly asked, leaning forward.

'Not very well, Miss... Lilly. But I'm learning.' Mary almost held her breath, waiting for what came next. Would Lilly laugh at her, call for her mother, or dismiss her like so many had before?

Lilly gave her a long, searching look. 'Rosamund has been helping, hasn't she?' Mary started at the question, eyes wide with surprise and fear. 'Don't worry. I'm glad. It seems I'm not the only girl here with a taste for knowledge.'

The admission landed softly between them, a tentative bridge. Mary stood still, trying to understand this change in her world. Lilly had known all along, and far from telling tales, she welcomed it. Mary's heart swelled with gratitude and hope, feelings she had taught herself to keep in check for so long.

Lilly leapt down from the desk. 'Mother thinks I've got too much education already. She won't hear of university, but I'm going anyway.' She drew a breath and smiled brightly at Mary. 'Perhaps you could borrow a book or two while I'm there.'

Mary's mind spun with the wonder of it. She longed to seize the offer, to lose herself in a hundred more words and worlds. But fear still shadowed her, the risk of losing everything if she was found out.

'I've not met another girl here who wants to learn,' Lilly said, as if sensing her hesitation. 'Take the books. Just don't let Mrs Goode catch you with them.'

Mary nodded. 'Lilly… do you think…' She bit her lip, then tried again. 'Could I ask a big favour of you?'

Lilly raised an eyebrow. 'What sort of favour?'

'I... I want to send a letter. To a friend. He's still in the Cripplegate Workhouse. But I can't risk sneaking out. Could you send it for me?'

'Sure! Would you like me to help you write it?'

'If you don't mind.'

'Let's get it done now that there's no one around.'

Lilly pulled a sheet of paper from the drawer and handed her a pencil. Mary took it carefully, her fingers brushing the wood. She hesitated. What if Sam never read this? What if he was already gone?

*Sam,*

*I don't know if you'll ever read this, but I have to try.*

*Are you safe?*

*I think of you every day. It's strange, being here. I'm in service now.*

*I wish I could tell you everything, but I don't even know where to start. Would you believe it if I said I was learning? Like reading and medicines.*

*I wish you were here. But more than that, I hope you're somewhere better soon.*

She hesitated, the tip of the pencil hovering over the paper.

*Not alone now.*

She sat back, staring at the words. Would Sam think she had forgotten him? That she was happy while he was still trapped in Turner's jail? She pressed her lips together, then slid the paper toward Lilly.

'I have to go out soon. I'll make sure this reaches him.'

Mary exhaled in relief. 'Thank you, Lily. That's very kind of you.'

Mary returned to the scullery with her head full of titles, and suddenly the mountain of chores ahead did not seem so steep.

Lilly and Mary took every chance they could to speak, their whispered words quick and careful as if carried on the wind. As secretive as spies in their own home. Mary learned of Lilly's bold dreams, of a world beyond her own imagining. Lilly's brother was more the favourite; Lilly knew this. She knew, too, that it would not change. Her fate was sealed, she said, unless she made her own way.

'Rosamund told me to find strength in myself,' Mary confessed one afternoon. Lilly's courage gave her the confidence to speak of such things. 'She said there's nothing I can't learn.'

Lilly's eyes brightened at this. 'And you believed her,' she said, approvingly. She pressed Mary's hand as they parted. 'I do too.'

# CHAPTER 11

*A*nd so it went, each day unfurling new possibilities that Mary had not thought were hers to have. Until the day it all fell apart.

The moment it happened was imprinted on Mary's memory as clearly as if it were etched there by a hot iron. She was carrying an armful of linens past the drawing-room when Lady Branscombe's voice cut through the air like a whip. Rosamund's name came first, then hers, then a torrent of words that turned Mary cold.

Rosamund was dismissed without ceremony, her few possessions gathered in haste. She stood on the step, her case at her feet, looking frail and resolute. Mary dared to beg for her to stay, tears burning tracks down her cheeks.

'Get back to work, you ungrateful girl!' Lady Branscombe struck her with the sharpness of a slap and a cold warning. 'You'll be on the streets as fast as your nurse, if I see another hint of trouble from you.'

Mary did not even feel the sting. Her heart was breaking for the loss of Rosamund, of the friend and mentor who had set her on this new path. She watched, helpless, as walked away.

The house felt emptier than ever with Rosamund gone. Mrs Goode grumbled as she shouldered the duties of both housekeeper and governess, her complaints punctuating every room.

'Three girls I need,' she announced to no one in particular, 'and it's just me doing it all.' Her bitterness fell on deaf ears. Lady Branscombe ignored her protests.

Mary drifted through the days, the bright fire inside her reduced to embers. She kept to herself, afraid to speak to Lilly for fear that she would be sent away next. She had known loss before, but each new blow seemed harder than the last.

It was Lilly who reached out, slipping a book into Mary's laundry pile, a message tucked between its pages. 'Rosamund would not want you to stop,' it said. 'Nor do I.'

They found ways to meet again, more cautiously than before. Lilly was not a nurse, but she was everything else Mary needed right now. Her knowledge filled the spaces that Rosamund's departure had left empty, and though they avoided being seen together, Mary felt Lilly's presence everywhere. In the logic of the sciences, and in the worlds she discovered within the pages Lilly gave her.

'If Mother knew,' Lilly said one day, a rare worry in her voice.

'She won't.' Mary knew now how to keep secrets, how to hide them in plain sight.

And so they conspired, and so Mary learned. Not just the stories the pages told, but what it took to chase them. She read late into the night, Rosamund's scraps still tucked inside her apron. She spoke the terms aloud, a faint whisper in the dark.

When she returned the book, another waited for her. 'I

think you'll enjoy this one,' said Lilly, the inscription in the looped handwriting that Mary could now read. 'With love. From a friend.'

The chapter closed with Mary alone in the laundry room, tracing her finger along the words Lilly had given her. They were still difficult, still strange. But a smile curved her lips. She would not stop learning. Never.

# CHAPTER 12

'Mary!' The word burst from Sam. He remained in the yard long after the rattle of the cart took her out of earshot. It was only when the incessant bell rang again that Sam turned his back and faced his life alone again. Two weeks on, and the lack of Mary still lay like a new wound inside him, which was why, when a sour-smelling man in a frayed coat came to the workhouse door looking for a boy, Sam let him rise to his feet and follow. If he could not have the joy of their escape, he might at least take their vow of freedom.

He huddled at the back of the wagon. The name Clemens had meant nothing to him, but Turner's parting words still hung in his mind. 'Perhaps your little friend will tend to you when she hears what became of you. If you make it long enough.'

The wagon lurched to a stop in front of a narrow building, taller than it was wide, with smeared windows and a worn stone step. A printer's shop. Sam took it all in as Clemens shouted at him to get down and to get on with it, then shoved him through the door.

'Worthless lot at the workhouse,' he grumbled, shaking his head. 'Scarecrows is all they send me.'

The sharp sting of ink closed in on Sam as he ducked inside. The shop was crowded with churning machinery. Boys like himself scrambled about with black hands and eyes flat with exhaustion.

'Oi, Sam! Over here!' Clemens was already down the length of the shop. Sam dashed after him and tripped on loose boards that seemed to want him sprawled on the floor.

'I won't have you lazy,' Clemens said when Sam stood in front of him. 'You work hard, or you're out. Don't care a bit. Many's the boy just waitin' for your spot.'

A boy beside Clemens snorted as he loaded typesets. 'Just in from the workhouse, are you? Better keep up, or you'll be under a cart by week's end.'

'Not if he keeps his wits,' Clemens shot back. He jerked his head toward the other boy. 'Do as Matthew tells you.'

Sam nodded and took his place beside Matthew.

The week crawled by, endless, each day blurring into the next, with Clemens prowling like a fox, nipping at their heels. Sam's fingers grew rough and clumsy. His sleep was shallow and dreamless, a snatch here and there in the hours Clemens grudgingly spared. Always, he was in demand; always, he was running; never, not for a moment, was he quick enough.

Sam caught what he could from Matthew, observing and mimicking. When Matthew slipped a cold potato from his shirt to eat for supper, Sam did the same. When Matthew ducked his head to avoid Clemens' fury, Sam learned to bend lower still. By the week's end, he had begun to keep pace.

Then, on the Sunday, Clemens saw him pause for a gulp of air. 'Slack! Slack, all of you! Just look at this, sittin' about like lords!' He swatted at Matthew, though Matthew was nowhere near where Sam had been.

'Wasn't me, sir,' Matthew yelped, ducking from the reach of the hand. 'It was him!'

'No, it wasn't,' said a little boy, thin as a needle, pointing straight at Sam.

Clemens rounded on Sam, and Sam did not flinch, not even as the printmaster's hand came within inches.

'You think you're a bold one, eh?' Clemens said. 'We'll see about that.'

From that moment on, Sam found himself beneath the lens of Clemens's cruelty. No matter how well he carried out his tasks, Clemens berated him, drove him, made him see the lash of the words. The days grew longer, harder. Sam felt his strength fail.

'I'll last the week, I will,' he said aloud.

'No one cares if you don't,' the needle-thin one told him. He shivered constantly with a cough that seemed a decade old. 'We all end up the same, one way or the other.'

Sam took a hard crust from his pocket and handed it to him. 'I'm not ending up that way.'

The boy turned his face to the wall, clutching the crust and coughing it to damp crumbs. His smallness made Sam ache, a different wound to the lack of Mary, but a wound all the same.

The next morning, Sam stood at his station. The little one was slower today, and Sam noticed his struggle. As the hour to finish neared, Sam dared a glance at him. He saw Clemens coming down upon him, knew the weight of it before Clemens opened his mouth, and shouted his defiance across the whir and churn of the shop.

'Not this time!' Sam said.

Then the slap came, its crack louder than the presses. Sam fell to his knees and felt the dust grind into him and the tears spring to his eyes. Tears, hot with fury. The boy's own quiet crying reached him, lost beneath the new scarlet of

Clemens's voice, the voice that went on and on and turned Sam's anger into fuel.

'Tonight,' Sam thought. 'Tonight, and I'll run for it.'

The minutes felt like hours, but at last, Sam lay awake among the others, breath held, ready. Clemens was a boulder in the office, snoring loud and reckless. He slipped past Matthew's sleeping body as he made his way out the door into the night air. Into freedom.

# CHAPTER 13

*L*ondon lay coiled in darkness, a breathing monster wrapped in the usual fog, and Sam walked its spine with no sign of pursuit. Whitechapel rose before him, the rotted teeth of its factories gnawing at the sky, a place where the wind snapped mean through the streets. He could hear the muffled howls from its alehouses. He kept on, slipping through the shadows with his thin jacket drawn close. There were eyes on him, he knew – eyes everywhere – but he didn't care. Let them see. Let them know he didn't fear their world.

He stumbled over cobblestones slick with the grime of a day's work, his feet carrying him to where he didn't know. Anywhere was better than Clemens's. A harsh bark of laughter echoed from an alleyway, followed by the sound of breaking glass. Sam kept his pace, unflinching. He imagined the headlines when they found him cold and stiff in the morning. 'APPRENTICE TURNED COLD PRINTER,' they would say, 'STARVED OF INK AND WAGES.' Perhaps that would make Clemens choke. Perhaps it would do him some good.

Ducking his head against the bitter wind, he turned a corner, the glowing maw of a tavern greeting him with warmth and noise. 'The Spotted Dog,' it said. He pushed the door with his shoulder and disappeared inside.

The place was alive with heat and the stink of stale ale mingled with sweat and the oily breath of lamps. Smoke drifted above the crowded tables where rough, loud men sat hunched over mugs. Sam edged his way to a corner, keeping his back to the wall, his presence as silent as a stray mutt. He dropped onto a bench and let his head fall into his arms.

'Not seen you here before, lad.'

Sam raised his eyes to find a man watching him from the next table. The stranger was older, with a sharp, curious look in his eyes. He wore the air of one at ease, even in this den of squalor.

'Bit young for the Dog, aren't you?' the man continued. 'Don't look like you've seen fourteen years yet.'

Sam didn't answer. His stomach was a hollow drum, throbbing with the ache of emptiness, and he wished for a moment that it would swallow the rest of him.

'Have a pint, then. Might warm you a bit.' The man shoved a mug toward him.

Sam eyed the drink, his fingers itching with the want of it. 'I haven't got…'

'Keep your coin,' the man interrupted. 'I'll wager you've none to spare.' He slid the mug closer. 'There's bread and cheese here, too. Go on. Before I change my mind.'

Sam snatched the food as though it might disappear, tearing into the bread with the ferocity of hunger. The first bite almost choked him; he had to slow himself to swallow.

'That's the spirit.' The man smiled. 'You from round here?'

Sam wiped the back of his hand across his mouth. 'I'm from everywhere.'

'Everywhere, is it? Well, it don't sound too far from nowhere. How'd you end up at the Dog?'

The noise in the pub swirled around them, a sea of drunken shouts and muttered arguments. Sam closed his eyes for a moment, letting it pull him under.

'Run away, did you?' the man pressed. 'That what brought you here?'

'No. Not running.'

The man leaned back, his expression still curious, still patient. He sipped from his own mug, watching Sam from under his eyebrows. 'Mind a name?'

Sam shrugged.

'Warren,' the man said. 'Oliver Warren. I'd say it was a pleasure, but you haven't got to the part where you talk yet.'

'Clemens,' Sam said, chewing on the name as he might a bitter root. 'I was working for Clemens. A printer.'

Oliver raised an eyebrow. 'And?'

'He's a bastard. There wasn't enough to eat, and it was colder inside than out. So I left.'

Oliver nodded. 'Thomas Clemens. That explains a deal.' He leaned in closer, his voice dropping to a conspiratorial whisper. 'No place for a young lad, that print shop of his. No place at all.'

Sam kept his eyes on the tabletop.

'How about a real roof over your head, then? Instead of Whitechapel's finest gutters?'

Sam's heart kicked, cautious and wanting. 'What are you on about?'

'I've a press in Spitalfields,' Oliver said. 'We print what the others won't. Real stories, real truth. The press runs hot, the beds are dry. Could use a smart lad to help out. Interested?'

Sam felt the gnaw of doubt. Things didn't turn like this. Not in his world. 'Why would you?'

Oliver held up a hand to silence him. 'Let's call it charity if you like, or call it luck. Either way, there's room for you. My apprentice left me for some fetching young thing, so I'm short of help. A few coppers in your pocket, maybe a square meal now and again – if you're good.'

Sam met Oliver's gaze, the older man's expression as sincere as it was strange. He felt a flicker. It was fragile, that flicker. Like the flame of a spent match. But he reached for it, tentatively, as though it might burn him. 'I can run ink and fix type. Sweep the floors. I can do whatever's needed,' he said, words tumbling out with breathless speed.

Oliver chuckled. 'I don't doubt it.' He drained the rest of his pint, then rose from the bench, motioning for Sam to follow. 'Let's be off, then. The night's no younger than you are.'

Sam trailed behind, weaving through the press of bodies. His eyes lingered on the promise of something new. When the door swung shut behind them, the cold caught him like a fist. He was still hungry, but now it didn't hurt so much.

The days stretched out with the warmth and clatter of Oliver's place. Ink stained Sam's hands instead of the thin grime of soot and cold, and he took to it gladly. They kept him busy. Running proofs to clients, delivering papers to newsboys on street corners, setting up type for the next issue. But it was honest work, and the pay, meagre as it was, felt like a fortune after Clemens's pit.

There was laughter here, and light, and talk of things he'd never imagined. Revolution, they said. Labour rights. The future, with words bold and ink smudged. It set fire to the ideas he'd barely dared to dream. Sam soaked it all up like a man who'd been thirsting his whole life.

He could see himself changing. It was in his face when he caught his reflection in the shop window. In the weight he'd gained. It was in the way he slept. Deep and long, instead of curled against cold hunger. Oliver teased him about it. Called him the best-fed newsboy in London, a rake with a bent for printing. Sam pretended to mind, but secretly he savoured every word.

There was something else, too. Like a string pulled tight across a distance. It vibrated softly, playing the same sad note until it was a part of him. It was Mary's absence, as haunting and heavy as it can get. When she filled his thoughts, he felt a pang like that first bite of bread, sudden and shocking in its need.

But this time, Sam wouldn't choke on it. He'd feed it with his own determined hands.

# CHAPTER 14

*A* splash of suds greeted Mary's bare feet as the metal bucket clanged loudly against the floor. Her heart thudded as if she had dropped that instead. She glanced around. No one seemed to have heard, so she tucked a lock of dampened hair behind her ear, grinned, and fell back into rhythm with the other scullery girls. The worn sleeves of her dress dripped onto the flagstones, soaking her hem and the soft, calloused skin of her toes. When she leaned forward, her wide eyes reflected in the water, catching the sharpness of her cheekbones and the new maturity of her fifteen-year-old features. She saw, with surprise, the delicate beauty the years had granted her. She saw also her future in the glistening pails and never-ending stacks of porcelain and silver.

Mary had grown accustomed to this life, though there was little joy in the constant scrubbing and polishing that filled her days. She set her hands to work while her mind wandered elsewhere.

Jack Branscombe had returned home recently, not from far, just from school. At first, Mary was no more than one of many faceless servants in his house. Now, Lily's brother lingered with a smile or a word for her, leaving Mary more puzzled than flattered by the sudden attention.

'Dreaming again, Mary?' called a girl across the room, laughing as she hauled a heavy pot from the floor.

Mary splashed more water on the floor, unable to hide her grin this time. 'Only dreaming this job was over.' She poured the water and tackled the next pile of dishes. No matter how endless the work, she was glad to be here rather than anywhere else. She had Lilly to thank for that. And although she was already off at university now, all those hours they'd spent together gave her a chance that girls like her rarely received.

Even after the arguments with her mother, after telling Lilly that she was foolish for teaching someone of her sort, she let Mary stay. She called her a wayward girl. She said the same of her daughter. And Mary did her best to repay their defiance in every ounce of strength she had.

An hour later, Mary headed up the stairs with a fresh load of laundry. She had almost reached the top when a young man's voice halted her in her tracks.

'You must be working very hard.' Jack smiled as if they shared some secret, something no one else was to know.

'There are always things to do here,' she said, uncertain if she should stop or keep moving. She decided to keep moving.

'I am glad to see you, Mary.'

Her heart fluttered at the sound of her name, but she forced a small laugh. He let her pass without expecting a reply.

Jack was the apple of his mum's eye, as Lily had said. He was the kind of boy who had always got what he wanted. At least, that's what Mary thought when she saw him next. She'd barely set a foot into the parlour before he started making excuses to help her. It began with a book.

He had caught her in the drawing room, cleaning the windows.

'Is that the sort of thing you like, Mary?'

She blushed, hoping his mother was nowhere near. 'It belongs to your sister. I was just putting it away.'

'Would you like to borrow it?'

Mary shook her head, feeling silly for thinking it might cause trouble. 'No, thank you. I don't think...'

'Then take it,' Jack said. 'Please. Lilly won't mind.' He reached across her, his sleeve brushing against her shoulder. Mary pulled away, uncertain if it was by accident.

'I'm sure she won't, but I've plenty to read already.'

She escaped the room as quickly as she could. It had become a game between them; she thought. She avoided him. He sought her. But something in Jack's eyes made Mary uneasy, a keen interest that went beyond mere friendliness.

When Jack offered to assist her with the silver a few days later, Mary refused as politely as she could. He was curious about her, asking questions about the work and her past. She felt strange about all of it and would have been suspicious if it had been anyone else but Lilly's brother.

'Wouldn't you like a hand with that?' he asked as she struggled with an armful of linens.

'I'm sure you've better things to do than follow me about,' Mary replied, trying to keep her tone light. But it was difficult when she knew she wasn't wrong.

'There is nothing better than this.'

She would have laughed if he hadn't looked so serious. When Jack's persistence continued to grow, Mary couldn't help but feel a chill beneath the warm glow of his attention.

'Mary!'

Her hand paused on the bannister, and she glanced back. She thought she heard Lilly's voice.

'Up here,' Jack said from somewhere above her.

When she reached the landing, he was waiting for her in the library, leaning against the door frame in a way that made her uneasy. It felt wrong. It felt forbidden. It felt as though they were children whispering things they shouldn't.

'I've been waiting for you, Mary. Come in for a minute.'

Her feet hesitated, knowing she shouldn't stay but curious about why she was there at all.

'I'm busy.'

'Please. We've hardly talked today.'

It was a truth that hit Mary with an intensity she wasn't expecting. She'd thought of him lately more than she cared to admit. And it was more than just the wrongness. It was how the wrongness had been buried with the rest of her past and how Sam hadn't written back. Lilly swore she'd sent his letter.

'What is it?'

'You don't have to be afraid.'

'I'm not afraid,' she said, walking into the room.

Jack was no longer smiling. He looked at her in a way that made her feel exposed, the gaze of someone who saw too much. Too much and not enough at the same time.

'I've been meaning to tell you. I like you.'

Mary shifted uneasily. 'You don't even know me.'

'I'd like to.'

She knew she should leave, but something in his voice was pleading and kept her where she stood. 'But why?'

Jack hesitated for a moment, as though weighing his answer carefully. 'Because you're not like the others. Because you're you.'

He stepped closer. Mary took a step back.

'It's not right.'

'Why not? We've nothing to be afraid of.'

'It's wrong. I can't. I won't.'

'Then don't. But you'll change your mind.'

Mary had been about to leave, had turned towards the door when he said it, but she paused long enough to look back and see him smiling. It made her angry. It made her ashamed.

She didn't hear him call after her. She was already gone.

'Mary,' he said, 'come up. Quickly.'

Jack's room. The words were spoken softly and with no hint of what they would mean.

'Jack?' Mary asked.

She stood now before the ajar door, a flutter of apprehension and something else stirring inside her. She had not wanted to come, but she couldn't bear the thought of making him angry. If she stayed away, Lady Branscombe would surely know. She would be dismissed. All she had done, all she had achieved, lost.

She gathered her courage and pushed the door gently. The room was empty. She heard a rustle of fabric and was about to turn back when she felt his presence behind her.

'Mary,' Jack said again, her name catching in his throat.

She could think of nothing to say, could barely think at all, and before she knew what was happening, Jack had closed the door and was drawing near.

'I've missed you.'

Mary's heart raced. Her eyes darted to the window, the way outside.

'I can't.'

'You can.'

This time, she did not step away. She wanted to. She

wanted to shout. She wanted to do a thousand things, none of which she could do because the world seemed to shrink around her, and she felt a terror she had not felt since her life was torn apart and she was a child of twelve in a place as grand as this. He touched her cheek; he moved closer, and suddenly, he was kissing her.

Her hands fell to her sides in shock and confusion, helpless as she stood and did not know what to do.

'Jack!' she cried, breaking free.

But the voice was not her own.

Lady Branscombe appeared before her, eyes blazing. Mary's breath came in shallow gasps, and she staggered back.

'M-m-mother.'

'This is how you reward my generosity?'

'I... no,' Mary said.

Lady Branscombe's lips curled into a sneer. 'Your wretched ingratitude. I see it clearly now. Do you really think you'll trap him with these sordid little games? I should have expected as much from the likes of you.'

Mary shook her head.

'I had no idea, mother. She's been following me everywhere.'

Lady Branscombe's eyes burned into Mary's, daring her to argue, to defy, to protest. But she could not. She stood frozen, numbed by the sudden ruin of everything.

The air was suffocating as Mary stood outside, watching the servants move busily through the house. They pointed, they stared, they whispered.

Mary waited at the gate for the carriage that would take her away, away from the house, from the injustice, from Lilly and the small hope she'd allowed herself to feel for a life beyond this one. A respectable life. An honest life.

But Mary knew it would never be all right again. Not if

she returned to Cripplegate, not if she lost what little dignity she had left.

Not if Sam had really forgotten her.

She thought of the possibility of seeing him again. But Mary knew she would never find him now, not there at the workhouse, not anywhere.

A man wearing a heavy coat and a grimmer expression approached the gate.

'Mary Bennett?'

She hesitated, glancing back at the house one last time.

'I've no more to wait. If you want your place there, you'll come along now.'

But Mary didn't want her place there. Not if it meant reliving all she'd fought so hard to escape. Her legs trembled as she took a step, as she turned away from the house and away from the man and away from the ruin and the pain and the awful, awful way the past had returned to break her in two.

She left the carriage waiting at the gate and did not look back.

# CHAPTER 15

$\mathcal{I}$n his heart, Mary was still there, though the work and bustle of his new life demanded he snuff her out. Every article Sam pressed for Oliver, every ink-stained page, seemed to mock him with its crisp certainty. How was she? He couldn't bear it. It was agony in the cruelest form.

The night after Mary left Turner's prison, while he was sleeping off his brandy, Sam had crept into his office. The ledgers lay open, pages thick with sealed fates – children sent to service, bodies lost to factory walls. And among them, he had found her.

*Mary Bennett – Branscombe House, 66 Blooms Crescent.*

'I can't shake her. I've got to find her, Oliver.' And he had, for his own peace, or what little the East End might afford. Sam threw off his apron and rushed to the door, hope trailing him like smoke, not knowing the address he had for Mary was gone as surely as she was from his life.

'Look here, Sam. You're losing your wits over this girl.'

Sam didn't care. He only nodded, a pleading earnestness in his eyes. 'Just a day, Oliver. A single day.'

The older man shrugged, offering a half smile. 'A day it is, then. But see you return in one piece.'

Sam barely heard him. He was already half out the door, Mary's name a persistent drumbeat in his chest. The districts of London closed around him as he cut through the streets. East, Central, and then West. Hope clung to him still throughout his journey.

Lady Branscombe's house rose from the haze with its grand facade, far removed from the sooty streets and despair of the East End. The brass knocker felt cold under Sam's anxious hand, and it was a long moment before the door creaked open. A sharp-eyed woman stood there, hands folded in a manner both prim and practiced.

'Madam,' he said.

'It's Mrs Goode, young boy.'

'I'm sorry, Mrs Goode. I'm looking for Mary. Mary Bennett. She is in service here, and...'

She interrupted with a thin, disdainful smile. 'Was.'

'Was? What do you mean by that? Is she...'

'Gone, yes. Gone without meeting the trust Lady Branscombe put in her. You should know her type, son.'

The accusation was an unspoken sneer, and Sam felt his stomach lurch. 'What do you mean?'

'Dismissed,' she said, with a kind of satisfaction. 'The girl seduced young Jack. Or so he says.'

Sam's head spun. 'And you believed him?'

'What I believe doesn't matter. She never boarded the carriage back to that place she came from. For all we know, she's turned street girl by now.'

Sam recoiled as if struck. The world, bright with possibility a moment before, collapsed around him. He saw the disdain on Mrs Goode's face, the slow closing of the door. He saw Mary, lost to him forever. The cobblestones felt uncertain under his feet, but still he ran.

~

For Mary, there was only shame. It had come crashing over her like the tide, relentless and drowning. The scene of her dismissal played over in her mind. Jack's insolent smile as he left her room would not be easy to forget. The injustice of it seared her heart. Mary stumbled through the streets, clutching a small bundle to her chest. Everything she owned. Everything she was.

She couldn't bear it. The hope she had nursed so carefully had shattered, leaving her raw and exposed to the world's cruelty. She was homeless. She was nothing.

It was the rejection she could not escape. She wandered, footsore and heartsick, a figure adrift in the uncaring swell of the city. Without references, she was unwanted, invisible to all who mattered. Mary moved through streets as flashbacks invaded her – intrusive, unbidden memories that caught her breath like a fist to the throat. Lilly's voice, frantic and far away. As far as she was after she left for university. Mary did not get her chance to say goodbye.

Mary felt abandoned to a fate as harsh and cold as the cobbled streets beneath her. She returned to herself by the docks. It had drawn her, this place, as if the docklands' silent, stretching expanse mirrored the depths of her own despair. Everything she had run from now closed in – her father's unjust arrest and death, her mother's slow fading away. Tommy's small body, burning with fever. Their spectres haunted her, all of them demanding she join them, finish what her broken heart had begun.

'Nothing left,' she whispered into the night. 'No future. No family. No...' She choked on the last words. They felt sharp, like glass in her throat. 'No Sam.'

Desperate, she moved closer to the water's edge, drawn by its dark, silent promise. The world blurred around her, memories folding into a nightmare that was both past and present.

Her mind spun back to the long-ago comfort of her father's arms, to the vibrant dreams he'd spun before the truth came to light. Before Mr Turner had robbed them of everything. 'New start,' he'd said, his voice brimming with the certainty of the young and hopeful. 'The docks, Mary girl. We'll make our fortune yet.'

Now they echoed back as taunts, cruel and empty. It was here, after all, that she had first understood what it meant to lose, to truly lose. Mary teetered on the brink.

But as she balanced there, the last scraps of courage leaving her, a new memory came flooding in. Her mother's kind hands, the way they'd smoothed the hair from her face, showed her how to hold on when everything else slipped away. 'Be strong,' they'd said. 'Be brave.' But could she? Did she even want to try?

Mary stepped closer to the edge, and closer still. The void seemed to welcome her.

The final moments came as clarity, all fear and doubt stripping away. There was nothing but the vastness of despair, and she was ready, more ready than she'd ever been in her fifteen short years.

She closed her eyes.

# CHAPTER 16

$\mathcal{M}$ ary didn't hear the clatter of carts from the street or the foghorns from the black river. Her mind, her heart, her bones were deaf to everything but the silent call of the water below. The step from this cold world seemed an easy one.

Then, a voice cut cleanly. 'What are you playing at, miss?'

Mary felt a touch on her arm and spun, finding herself face to face with a girl who seemed hardly more than a child. She wore a patched coat and a sincere expression, with cheeks smudged by the day's work at the factory. 'Best come along. Unless you're one of them mermaids.'

Mary hesitated, the words catching at her like thorns. The other girl saw her waver and pressed on.

'There's room if you don't mind a bit of company.'

Mary shivered in its damp chill. What did it matter now? She thought of the emptiness drifting through a world where warmth and love had turned their backs. A soul who didn't belong. What was she meant to do when everything she touched slipped away? What did anything matter anymore?

'I...'

'I'm not stopping you,' the girl continued. 'But I'd be right sad if you did it.' She released her grip, but her eyes stayed fixed on Mary's.

Another moment stretched like wire between them, then snapped. Mary moved a step away from the edge, then another.

'There you go, now. Best get along home. Where's that, then?'

Mary didn't answer. Her silence filled with the memories of everywhere she had been, and the thought that she belonged in none of those places. Lady Branscombe's door slamming on her heels. Rosamund with tears in her eyes, offering no help or hope or home.

'You're like me, I reckon. Not one place or the other,' the girl said, reading the silence easily. 'Come on then, keep me company.' She nodded back toward the foggy streets, and this time Mary followed.

They walked in silence for some time, Mary's breath puffing in pale clouds as they hurried through darkened alleys and past tall factories looming like giant iron men. It was late, and few were about in this part of London, though the night watchman's lantern threw an occasional flicker onto their path. Mary trailed the other girl with a dragging gait, as if every step tugged at the roots of her misery. In a courtyard off a narrow street, they stopped in front of a soot-streaked door.

'It's a bit of a squash,' said the girl, 'but better than the Thames. Come with me.'

The room was crowded with cots, bodies wrapped in blankets, and clothes hung up to dry. It was crowded, but not cold, and the warmth of the place struck Mary after the chill of outside. There were girls everywhere – on the floor, on chairs, their hair still wet from washing – and they all looked up when the pair entered.

'Eh, what's this?' said one, sitting up and peering through the dim light.

'Thought I'd bring us another mouth,' said the girl. 'Or another pair of hands.'

They laughed at this and made space for Mary. It was strange, the feeling of being welcome. It rubbed against the rawness of her recent loss. She hovered by the door, a little afraid to come all the way in.

'She's one of them shy ones,' said a small girl with her hair in plaits.

'She'll learn different here,' said another. 'C'mon then, no use letting the flies in.'

The girl with the plaits laughed. 'Leave off, she's half froze!'

Mary felt a gentle hand take hers and pull her inside.

'Thanks,' she said in a low voice. She glanced at the girl who had found her.

'I'm Nellie,' the girl said. 'That's Susie,' she nodded to the girl with the plaits. 'And Meg and Annie and – well, you'll learn us soon enough. Sit yerself down.'

Mary found herself sitting with the girls, their faces alive with curiosity. She thought of them with dullness that would not lift. Girls who were sisters to each other, and would never know the loss she knew.

'She's a bit tired-like, aren't you?' Nellie gave her a warm look. 'You rest up. Got something for you.'

Mary watched Nellie bustle about the crowded room, her hands deft and sure. After some minutes, she returned, holding out a cup.

'It's only tea,' she said, pressing it into Mary's hands. 'But better than nowt.'

Mary took it, grateful for the warmth that seeped through the cup and into her cold fingers.

'You look like you could do with a bit of supper, too. And

a proper night's sleep.' Nellie's voice was gentle, like Rosamund's had been. Like she wanted Mary to stay. 'Get that down you, and we'll see about a blanket.'

Mary wrapped her fingers tightly around the cup and nodded, feeling a strange sort of weakness creep into her. The kind that didn't come from being hungry or cold or even lonely, but from knowing it didn't have to be that way.

She found a corner and curled up with the cup, breathing the steam from the tea until her eyes grew heavy. The voices around her merged with dreams of Tommy, her parents, and the hollow rooms of her past until everything slipped away.

# CHAPTER 17

*T*he next morning, Mary woke to the sight of Nellie pulling on a threadbare coat.

'Best not run off if you don't want more tea chucked over you,' she said with a smile. 'We'll be back before dark. There's bread in the cupboard.'

The other girls were readying themselves for the day's work, talking over one another with tired voices and lively laughs. Nellie paused on her way to the door.

'You sure you'll be alright, then?'

Mary nodded, her voice still wrapped in sleep. She didn't quite trust it not to break if she tried to speak. She sat up and watched the girls leave, their chatter following them out onto the streets. The room was quiet for the first time since she'd been there, and she sat in the middle of it with the blanket pulled around her shoulders. The sun cut weak stripes across the walls, painting the morning with the shadow of window-panes. She pulled the cup of cold tea into her lap and stared at it.

The memories came fast and jagged, like glass on skin. Her father in his workshop, the smell of sawdust and glue and hope. Her brother Tommy. The sweet, sudden rush of him as a child.

'You'll see, Mary,' Tommy would say. 'It's all going to be different.'

She knew better. And now she knew it always would be.

There were three weeks of haunting the city with nowhere to go, wandering to forget and finding only that she was forgotten. She'd stopped expecting much of anyone. The days in the city left her raw, bleeding hope that wouldn't heal.

After the terrible shock of Rosamund's dismissal, after that last hopeful ride across town and the despair when she reached Lilly's and saw the looks on the other servants' faces, Mary could not think of a place she could go. That her best option had been the cold water at the docks. That even now, safe and warm in Nellie's lodging house, she still wasn't sure if the matchgirl's kindness could mend her or if she wanted it to.

Mary moved stiffly. She reached the cupboard where Nellie had pointed and found a few slices of bread, quickly going stale. She didn't mind. She ate one and wrapped the blanket more tightly around her shoulders. The room felt emptier without the girls. It reminded her too much of herself, and she shrank into her corner.

When the girls returned, Mary was surprised at how relieved she felt. Their noise, their presence, chased some of the hollow feeling away. They brought food with them – potatoes, bits of bacon, a half-eaten loaf – and made a small feast of it on the floor. Nellie was insistent that Mary eat until she felt she might burst. But the warmth in her stomach spread to other parts of her, parts she had thought were beyond warmth or care.

It was like this for many days. The girls left each morning and returned in the evening, and gradually, Mary began to feel less like an intruder among them. Her gratitude for Nellie was deep, though she had no way to repay the kindness except to help with supper and talk into the long hours when the girls were still awake enough to chat.

They were not so different from her; she learned. They worked in a match factory nearby, dipping the wooden sticks into phosphorous that turned their skin strange colours and made their breath smell sweet and sickly. The hours were long, and the wages barely kept them fed and housed. But they shared what little they had with a generous spirit that reminded her of Sam and – oh! – how different things could have been if the world were fair.

'You don't work?' Susie asked her one night, the way only a twelve-year-old can ask.

Mary smiled at the forthright question, touched by its innocence. 'Not yet.'

'Eh, you're lucky, then. Lucky as we come.'

But was she? Wasn't she also cursed by her luck? Cursed to survive when others she loved were gone?

Mary didn't say so. 'I'll not stay forever,' she said instead. 'You've been ever so kind. I can't be a burden for long.'

'Eh,' said Nellie, tossing her plaited hair like she did at the end of every shift. 'We like a bit of burden now and then. Keeps us strong.'

Mary remembered something Lilly once said about being lucky. 'You have people, Mary,' she had said. 'More than most, you do.'

More than most? It hadn't felt that way to Mary then, and it didn't feel that way now. Yet here were these girls, making room for her when they had none to spare, laughing with her as if she'd been part of their lives forever.

It struck Mary like a flash of fever – the sudden realisation that she had something she had lost. She was needed. Maybe only in a small way, a way that could be replaced by any other girl who wanted to pull her weight and share in the cramped warmth of this life. But it was a way. And in the absence of anything else, in the absence of everything she thought she'd have by now, Mary decided to try.

The next day, she wrapped her threadbare shawl tight and walked with the girls to the factory. She saw it from the outside first, the long rows of windows and the figures of workers moving behind the glass. Her heart began to thud painfully, the memory of workhouse doors and stone walls a sick echo in her mind.

'Not what you're used to, I reckon,' Nellie said as they drew near.

Mary hesitated. In some ways, it was – too much like the workhouse, too much like being trapped. But this was different. The walls might close in, but this time, she walked through the door.

The forewoman, a grey figure with a long nose and a voice that cracked like a whip, stopped Mary with a look. 'We don't take strays.'

'She's with us,' Nellie told her, and Mary was surprised at how much authority came through in the small voice. She glanced sideways at her, thankful.

The forewoman's lips pursed tightly. 'I'll dock you for her if she can't keep up. Get along, then.'

The day was as long as Mary expected, the air close and choked with chemicals. Her hands were soon stained with the red powder that dusted every surface, and her head began to spin with the smell. She sat with the girls and made boxes for the matches, watching how they moved their hands like nimble magicians.

'I'm right hopeless,' she said, after her tenth ruined attempt.

'Eh, you're getting the hang of it.' Nellie, like always, found encouragement where there was none to be had.

～

Weeks bled into months. Then years.

The rhythm of the factory became as familiar to Mary as the rise and fall of her own breath. The work was brutal, the wages still barely enough, but the matchgirls made it bearable. They had their small victories – laughing at the forewoman behind her back, finding joy in things the world told them they had no right to want.

Mary no longer struggled to keep up. She would be twenty soon, and had grown stronger. Her hands moved as deftly as the others, her fingers stained red like everyone else's. The factory air no longer made her dizzy. The phosphorous clung to her skin, her clothes, but she learned to live with it, just as they all had.

Even Susie, once the smallest among them, had grown. Her plaits weren't quite so tight anymore, and her laughter had lost the breathless, childlike shrillness it once had. But the work was cruel. And the price it demanded, relentless.

It was long past midday when it happened. Susie gave a little cough that didn't sound right, didn't sound like a cough at all. More like something caught. Something wet.

Mary looked at her, and in that moment all the work stopped. Susie's hand went to her mouth and came away streaked with blood, and the girls moved in a well-rehearsed panic.

'Get her out of here!' Annie shouted.

Mary caught Susie by the shoulders as Nellie opened the door.

'To the fresh air with her!' called the forewoman. 'The lot of you! Don't think you'll be paid for the hour!'

She hardly noticed the chill biting her cheeks after the heat of the factory. She held onto Susie and found herself running. They gathered in the courtyard of the lodging house, and Mary watched in helpless terror as the small girl writhed in pain. Her eyes went wide with a kind of fear she thought she'd never feel again – the fear that someone else she loved was dying. She couldn't. She wouldn't. Not now. Not like Tommy. Not when she finally felt alive.

'It's the phossy jaw,' Nellie said.

Mary cradled Susie's burning face, her fingers brushed along her jaw, searching. No crumbling bone. No rotting flesh. Not yet.

'Mary?' Nellie's voice wavered. 'Is it?'

'I am not sure, but it could be if she's not cared.'

'What do we do?'

'We need to cool her down and clean her up,' Mary said, already reaching for a cloth. 'And she needs a doctor before it gets worse.'

'Help me, Mary, it hurts,' Susie said.

She worked fast, pressing a damp cloth to Susie's lips, gently tipping her chin to keep her airway clear. She remembered Rosamund's hands – steady, never shaking. She tried to do the same.

'There now, Susie. Just a little longer.'

Susie whimpered but swallowed, letting Mary wipe away the worst of the blood.

The matchgirls huddled closer, their faces full of thanks and relief and amazement.

'We'll take her now,' Nellie said. 'No one's turning her away.'

'Eh,' said Nellie, squeezing Mary's shoulder. 'What did I tell you? We've a nurse among us.'

A nurse.

The word sent a jolt of something hot through her. Something strong. Something certain. How many years had passed since she'd dared to think it? Since she'd let herself want it?

She hadn't saved Susie, not really. But she had helped. And she would do it again.

She closed her eyes for a moment, feeling the weight of it, the shape of something new forming in her chest. Something she wished she could tell Sam.

It was not the end. It was the beginning.

~

The days stretched out, brighter now, with the small lodgings bursting at the seams. Mary, Nellie, and the others took turns nursing Susie back to health, and as they did, they took turns dreaming. Dreaming of what they'd do when they were rich, dreaming of what it might be like to live a life without factories and fires and the taste of phosphorous in the back of their throats.

Mary dreamt with them. And then she dreamt her own dreams. Of never having to leave. Of finding a way to keep this life. Of becoming the nurse she had once promised Tommy she would be.

And of Sam.

She wondered if he remembered her. If he knew that she'd survived when so many hadn't.

She wondered what she'd do if she saw him again.

And for the first time in too long, the thought didn't scare her. It wasn't loss, or longing, or something broken beyond repair.

It felt like possibility.

Like something she might mend.

# CHAPTER 18

Spitalfields, East London, 1885.

Emily had been part of Sam's life for years now, steady as the hum of the press, a quiet force he had come to rely on. Oliver's niece, sharp-minded and warm-hearted, had taken to the press like she'd been born to it. She and Sam worked side by side each day, their conversations easy, their silences never strained.

Tonight, she lingered by the door, watching him disappear into the streets. She loved him, in her gentle way, and was content to let him decide what lay ahead for them. She had a sense that his heart was not fully hers, but she would wait, believing that his unresolved feelings would soften in time. Emily turned back inside, her footfall silent as her thoughts, and let the press's steady rhythm fill the spaces in her mind where her uncertainties lingered.

'Emily, you'll run yourself ragged keeping pace with that boy,' Oliver called over the clanking of machinery.

She laughed lightly, her eyes still fixed on the door. 'Sam was late today.' She came to stand by Oliver, taking the bundle of papers from him. 'He works too hard, don't you think?'

Oliver grunted with affectionate exasperation. 'You defend him more than he deserves, Emily. If Sam Brown kills himself over this business, it's only his own fault.'

'He was quieter than usual today.'

'He's trying to forget, Uncle.'

Oliver sighed and lowered his voice. 'That little girl?'

Emily nodded. 'Wherever she is… if she still is, she's a grown woman now.'

They both fell into silence, their thoughts shadowed by the memory that seemed to haunt Sam.

Sam turned a corner, heading towards his narrow lodgings in Whitechapel. He moved briskly, driven by the cold or by his thoughts, not even he could tell. As he reached his door, a small figure emerged from the shadows, touching his arm hesitantly.

'Mr Brown?' the young boy asked.

Sam recognised him as a lad from the workhouse and tensed, already bracing himself for disappointment. 'Any news?' he asked, harsher than intended, placing a shilling in the boy's hand.

The question tasted like defeat. For years, he had searched – asking in the West End, the East End, following the dead trails she left behind. But London swallowed its lost whole. If she still lived, he had no way of knowing where. She could be anywhere, anyone.

The lad shook his head. 'No sign of her, sir. I'm sorry.'

Sam nodded, trying to mask his despair. 'Keep looking. Another shilling if you find anything.'

He watched the boy disappear before climbing the steps to his room. Once inside, Sam sank into the worn chair by the window, staring out into the grey void where Mary seemed to have vanished.

Whitechapel had swallowed them both. It should have been impossible – they walked the same streets, breathed the same soot-clogged air. And yet, in all these years, not a whisper of her. He had searched – God, how he had searched. Asking every workhouse lad with sharp eyes to earn a shilling. Nothing. Either she had left London, or she had learned how to disappear better than even he had.

His thoughts returned to Emily, to the warmth and kindness he couldn't fully embrace. He closed his eyes, trying to focus on Emily's face, but it was Mary he saw – frail, determined, her spirit unbroken despite everything. How could he explain to Emily that the memory of Mary was both a comfort and a curse? It pulled him back to the boy he once was, alone and helpless, yet it spurred him on, driving him to seek the justice they both believed in. But each failed attempt to find her deepened his fear that he had lost her for good.

Sleep did not come easily that night. Dreams of the workhouse, of Mary, of the promises they made, filled the restless hours. He awoke before dawn, determined to cast off the weight of these dreams. His mind was made up by the time he reached the press that morning. Emily greeted him with her usual sweetness, a hint of concern in her eyes.

'You look tired, Sam.'

He smiled, a bit wryly, determined to make light of his troubles. 'I'm just too much of a perfectionist, that's all.'

Oliver appeared from the back room, holding a proof sheet. 'Or a masochist,' he added, shaking the paper. 'Is it true what she says? You'll send yourself to an early grave working like this.'

Sam laughed, accepting the sheet from Oliver. 'Better an early grave than an empty one.'

Emily frowned slightly but kept her voice gentle. 'You push yourself too hard. You need a day for yourself, for all our sakes.' She glanced at Oliver for support, and the older man nodded, putting a firm hand on Sam's shoulder.

'She's right. You've earned it. Why don't you come to dinner tomorrow? Emily insists you remember that you're still human.' There was warmth in Oliver's teasing, and Sam felt a familiar tug of guilt mixed with gratitude.

'I'd like that,' Sam said, hesitating only a moment. 'And I'm sorry if I've been...' His voice trailed off.

Emily touched his hand, understanding without needing to hear. 'We know.'

Sam spent the rest of the day at the shop, burying himself in work to silence the voices that refused to leave him alone. As he set the type for the next issue, he wondered if he would ever manage to truly let go. Emily watched him from across the room, her love patient and undemanding. By evening, when Sam finally left, the streets of Spitalfields seemed to swallow him whole, a phantom among phantoms.

Oliver shook his head as he locked the door. 'Too hard on himself, that one. Just like you said, Emily.'

Emily watched the fog where Sam had vanished, feeling both close to him and impossibly far. 'He wants to let her go. I know he does. But it's himself he needs to let go of first.'

Sam walked the streets, lost in thoughts. The suggestion of dinner with Emily and Oliver lingered, both a comfort and a challenge. Could he be what Emily deserved? Did he even know what he wanted to be? He paused outside a gaslit pub, the warmth inside spilling onto the cobbles, and considered drowning his doubts in beer. But another figure at the bar, alone and waiting, turned him back to the streets. He was tired of waiting. He wanted answers, closure, peace. He returned to his cold room, determined to find them.

That determination brought him back to Emily and Oliver the next evening, resolved to at least try. He brought flowers, an old-fashioned gesture that made Emily blush with pleasure. Her delight was like a balm, soothing the raw places in his heart. Dinner was simple and comforting, the sort of meal he imagined families shared. They talked and laughed, Oliver spinning tales of the publishing world, Emily chiming in with sharp observations. For a while, Sam allowed himself to feel at home, allowed himself to believe he could belong there.

He saw Emily watching him, her eyes filled with a mixture of hope and understanding. She wasn't blind to his turmoil, but she offered him a refuge from it. The evening passed too quickly, and as he left, he felt a pang of loss, already missing the warmth.

Emily walked him to the door, hesitating before speaking. 'Will you be all right, Sam?'

'I'm getting there,' he said, giving her hand a squeeze. He wanted to promise her more, but words failed him.

'I believe in you,' she said, holding his gaze and letting him go with a tenderness that cut through his defences.

The air seemed lighter as Sam made his way home, lighter than it had been in a long time. He tried not to let doubt creep in, tried to remember Emily's faith in him. That night, he dreamed of Mary again. But this time she wasn't alone; Emily stood with her, their hands joined, their faces fading in and out of the shadows. He woke with a start, willing to put the past to rest. His steps led him back to the workhouse the next day, pursuing one last rumour, one last chance.

It was raining, the kind of persistent drizzle that soaked

through coats and spirits alike. Sam waited in a narrow alley, watching the comings and goings at the Cripplegate gates. He felt half mad with hope, convinced that this time he'd find what he'd been looking for. But as the hours passed, his hope thinned, worn away by rain and reality.

Another boy approached him, shivering and wide-eyed. Sam's heart leapt, ready to believe, ready for anything. 'Any news?' he asked, barely able to voice the words. The boy shook his head, drenched and uncertain. 'None, sir.'

Sam slumped against the wall, the weight of his unanswered questions pressing down. 'Keep looking,' he said, his voice raw and desperate. He gave the boy what he could spare, watching as he disappeared into the bleak afternoon. Mary felt further away than ever, more ghost than memory. He returned to Spitalfields, to the life that waited for him there, trying to convince himself that it was enough.

# CHAPTER 19

hree years later, all the bells in East End London seemed to have joined the call. It was a new day, and the streets filled with it. From the banks of the Thames to the grim courts of Whitechapel, the rumble grew as men and women poured out of workshops and factories. The bright air snapped with change, with rebellion, with banners aloft and voices clamouring for justice, their cries like nothing the city had ever heard. Women led the charge. Once pale and hungry in the match factories' grip, they surged now with the full force of the wronged, voices high and angry, feet relentless in their demand. It had started quietly years before – girls like Susie, lucky enough to escape the ravages of phosphorus, and girls like Meg and Annie, who hadn't been so fortunate. Their deaths had gone unanswered, their pain unnoticed, but not forgotten.

Onward, onward from street to street, they pressed, and with them, along the cobbles and under the shrouded sky, pressed the shouts of a thousand newsboys hawking their eager dispatches. From Cripplegate to Whitechapel and beyond, workers joined the march, and a young man cut his way among them. The journalists were out in droves. Sharp of eye and sharper of elbow, they jostled one another for the prize: the scoop of the decade.

'It's like a damned cattle market!' a moustachioed reporter grumbled as he pushed his way past.

Sam dodged him with a nimble step. 'Bit of an improvement, isn't it, Arnold?'

'You would say so, you rascal!' came the retort, but Sam was already gone, swallowed by the swarm of voices and motion.

The factories had birthed a beast. Women filled the streets, their dresses bright under layers of coal dust, faces set with fierce determination. Signs painted with 'FAIR TREATMENT NOW' and 'JUSTICE FOR OUR DEAD' danced above the crowd, while matchworkers – thin and weary but unyielding – cried for change.

Sam ducked past a vendor's cart, his pen and pad clutched tightly in one hand. Each word, each impression, he scribbled with urgency.

From the pavements and balconies, onlookers gaped at the scene. There was fear and fascination in their stares, the proper citizens unused to such uproar from the less-than-proper folk. In all the madness, Sam's heart beat with a pace to rival the marching feet, the thrum of it spurring him on.

'Samuel, you hound!' The shout broke through the tumult. A red-faced lad sprinted to catch up with him, panting as he fell into step.

'Frank! Thought you'd gone soft on me.'

Frank shot him a wry look, wiping sweat from his brow. 'More chance of me getting soft than this lot giving up.' He nodded towards the mob of protestors. 'They're on fire today. Right the way from Bow to here.'

'Good,' Sam said, breathless with it all. 'Someone needs to

be.' He darted ahead, leaving Frank shaking his head in admiration or disbelief – it mattered little which.

Whitechapel loomed ahead, its old brick tenements standing guard over the swelling throng. Workers spilled from the streets and alleys, joining in a great surge of bodies. With a pace that matched the day, Sam plunged further in, intent and relentless as the crowd itself.

Smoke rose like an angry shroud, but the spirits rose higher. The great human river poured onward, and Sam rode its current deeper into the heart of East End rebellion.

He had begun this morning with hopes of a front-page spread, but as he watched the workers around him, he saw more than headlines. Faces lifted with resolve, young girls too frail for their strength, women whose lives had been bought for a matchbox's worth of wages. Every line of their bodies, every note of their songs, spoke louder than anything he'd write, and the importance of it nearly swept him away.

Near Spitalfields, Sam hesitated, torn between two columns of chanting, banners, girls. A quick flash of doubt gripped him, sudden and stark, the fear of losing the trail, the story – the chance. It only took a moment, but that moment made him late.

'You're missing it, Sam! They're heading towards the bridge!'

A bandy-legged reporter caught his sleeve, half-dragging, half-pulling him back the way they'd come.

He cursed himself for not being faster, for losing precious time, for all the things that nearly slowed him, but none of them slowed him now. He moved like a man possessed.

He saw her, suddenly, there among the marchers. She was all grown, not a girl but a woman, taller and older than his memory allowed, and for an instant, his stride faltered, his breath caught.

Mary. It had to be her. He'd been a fool to believe it, to

think he'd find her after all this time, after all that had passed between them. But there she was, and the very impossibility of it made him certain.

He stood for half a heartbeat, stunned and unsure. She'd changed – how could she not? Her face was sharper now, the softness gone. But he'd know her anywhere, and the surprise of it filled him, every thought and nerve, filled him till he thought he'd burst.

Someone bumped against him, and the moment snapped. She was disappearing, swallowed by the crowd.

'Mary!' he shouted. His voice was nearly lost among the other cries.

She turned.

Her eyes met his, a brief connection, startled and questioning. Recognition and doubt battled across her features. Was it truly him, here, amidst all this?

She hesitated, and the world hung with her, poised to spin one way or the other.

Sam fought his way through, past bodies and banners, elbows sharp against his ribs. The noise of the protest beat at him from all sides, but he had no thought but this: to reach her, to hold her before she slipped away again, before she vanished like the ghost she'd been all these years.

How had she come to be here, in the thick of it, when he'd thought her lost to the world?

He felt a rising fear, an awful certainty that he'd lose her again. She was farther now, almost out of sight. He pushed harder, breathing hard and fast, thinking only of her, of their past, of a future he never dared to imagine till this moment.

Her face, that glimpse of it, burned like fire in his mind. Stronger now, fuller, driven by time and by labour, by causes she'd thrown herself into. By life, with or without him.

She'd been an orphan, like him. They'd known each other's pain. They'd been so close, so tangled in fate and ambition, and now here they were – so close again, but not close enough.

'Mary!' His voice came out broken, rough with hope and fear. She turned once more, then disappeared behind a throng of matchgirls.

He cursed the crowd, the streets, his own heart for daring to hope. For believing that he'd find her, that she'd still be – what? His? She never had been, not really.

Not before, when they'd been two lost souls in the Cripplegate Workhouse, sharing dreams and failures. Not after, when the past had cut them apart. But she was here, and that was enough.

He closed the gap, every step a fight. He'd nearly reached her when the world exploded in sound and motion. The crowd split and re-formed, thickening around him like a knot.

A shiver of doubt passed through Mary as she stared back at him, unsure. His face among the thousands. Could it be? The very thought made her shake. She tore herself away, more frightened of what she hoped than what she knew. And with the certainty that hope always came with pain.

The protest carried her forward, away from him.

# CHAPTER 20

$\mathcal{T}$he crowd had finally dispersed, drifting away into Whitechapel's maze of streets and alleyways, leaving behind only trampled banners calling for justice. Sam's heart pounded furiously in his chest as he followed her. He'd nearly lost her half a dozen times, her slender figure disappearing into the crowd, only to reappear again. Now she stood just ahead, near a narrow alley next to the matchgirls' lodging. Mary was chatting with the other girls, unaware of his approach.

He took a step forward and her name tumbled from his lips.

'Mary!'

She turned instantly, as if she'd been waiting for him all along, disbelief etched across her face.

'Sam?' Her voice trembled with emotions she'd long tried to bury.

A knowing smile flickered briefly across Nellie's face. She gently grasped Susie's arm and started guiding her away, murmuring softly, 'Come along, Susie. Let's give them a moment, shall we?'

Susie glanced back, curious, but Nellie pulled her gently down the street, leaving Sam and Mary alone in the quiet of the alleyway.

Mary hadn't moved, hadn't dared to breathe. 'Is it really you?' she managed at last.

Sam closed the distance between them, reaching out, afraid she might vanish again. His voice broke. 'Mary, I've been looking and looking...' He couldn't get the words out quickly enough. 'All of London. It's really you. Oh, Mary, it's really you.'

She still couldn't move, couldn't speak. The world around her echoed away. All of London, and yet there was nothing, no one – no one but Sam. He was right there, right in front of her.

It was everything; it was impossible.

'Mary,' he said again. He reached her, his arms coming around her and pulling her close. Her breath caught, as if it might stop altogether.

'I was terrified I'd lost you again in the protest,' he whispered against her hair, holding her as if she were air, precious and vital.

She saw every moment. Every hour, every year he thought he'd lost her. Her voice cracked. 'How are you here? How are you really here? I don't. I can't...' It was too much, far too much for mere words. She held on tighter, and the empty streets around them seemed to fall away.

They were scared, scared it wasn't real, scared it couldn't last. But not scared enough to let go.

They said each other's names again and again. Just that – just that and nothing else. Sam and Mary and the years and the hopes and everything.

They held each other for minutes that stretched endlessly, until at last, Sam broke the silence.

'Mary, I was terrified I'd never find you again. Where have you been?'

Mary pointed at the building right down the alley. 'I've been here in Whitechapel for years, working at the match factory. The girls were kind enough to let me stay with them.'

'You were here all along. So close. I don't live far from here, but spend my days working in Spitalfields.'

She laughed, choked on a sob, still not fully believing. 'It seems too easy now after everything.'

He held her tighter, truer. 'No,' he breathed, shaking his head. 'Not easy. I've been searching for years. I thought I'd go mad before I found you.'

'I didn't let myself hope. It seemed impossible.'

'You're not dreaming. Not this time.'

'I thought I'd never see you again.'

'Me too. Mary, oh… me too.'

She buried her face in his shoulder, holding onto him with every ounce of strength she had left.

The words kept coming, unstoppable, each one tumbling into the next. Sam pulled her closer still, afraid to lose her again.

'Sam, I thought you'd given up after…'

'Mary, I never stopped looking. Not even when you vanished from Lady Branscombe's. I went there and Mrs Goode told me what has happened with that boy.'

She felt the words. Words that reopened a wound that had closed. But that did not hurt anymore.

'That liar. He always got what he wanted and thought he could have me too.'

'I believed in you. I knew that wasn't the real story.'

She felt the words, felt the truth behind them, yet still couldn't quite believe. Her arms tightened around him. 'I thought you wouldn't care anymore.'

He drew back, meeting her eyes for the first time in what

felt like a lifetime. He saw the pain there, raw and familiar. 'Mary. I never stopped caring. Not for a moment.'

'I wrote you a letter before they… before she…'

'Oh God. Mary, I never got any letter.'

Her voice trembled with hurt and relief. 'I didn't even know if you'd received it.'

'I would've come,' he interrupted fiercely, desperately. 'I'd have come if I'd known.'

She finally knew, finally believed it completely. 'Sam, I'm so glad, so glad you didn't stop.'

They held onto each other in silence for a moment that seemed endless. He breathed her in, as if she were life itself.

'After everything,' he said softly, 'I thought…'

'I thought I'd lost you forever,' she finished for him.

He nodded, eyes shining with tears. 'I was afraid you'd think…'

'I know,' she said. 'I know.'

'That I'd stopped loving you.'

That word – she hadn't expected it. Perhaps she'd hoped, deep down, but never dared to expect. 'I never knew. Not even then.'

'Not even when we were too young to know what it was?' he asked.

She looked into his eyes; her own glistening with tears. 'I've always felt the same way about you.'

It was more than breath, more than air, more than all the years and all of London and all the time lost and found.

His voice broke fully now. 'Mary…'

She was crying; he was crying. It was laughter, it was tears, it was everything.

'I never let myself. I couldn't. I didn't even know…'

'After we were separated, after you were taken away. I thought…'

'Not even after that,' he said fiercely, drawing her close again. 'Not even then.'

They stood holding one another, alone in the quiet alley-way. Alone in the world.

Yet not alone at all. Not alone now.

'Mary. I've loved you from the first day.'

She held him tighter, unable to stop the tears.

They pulled each other closer, no more distance, no more empty spaces.

Just Mary. Just Sam.

'We're here,' he said. 'We're finally here.'

And they didn't stop holding.

He wouldn't let her go. Not now.

Not ever.

# CHAPTER 21

$\mathcal{E}$mily was wearing green for hope, the same shade she'd worn that evening months ago, when Sam had come with flowers, making her blush like a schoolgirl. That night he had smiled differently, laughed more freely. In the weeks that followed, he had even dared to kiss her softly on her doorstep. That kiss, gentle as it had been, had sustained her these past months, letting hope creep softly into her heart.

But the hope had faded to pale yellow the moment Sam stepped into the press following the aftermath of the protests. His eyes almost gave away the news she dreaded to hear.

Now she sat in the shabby little room, over tea she couldn't drink, her neat boots catching the edges of the worn rug, the thought catching her again and again that love shouldn't be this way, this tiresome, lonely little death. She arranged the cups with trembling hands, stared at the patterns of old light on the wall, imagined new futures in the shapes she saw there.

Sam walked down the corridor. 'Emily, we need to talk.' His voice snapped her heart to its most forlorn attention.

Oliver walked to the back of the press as soon as he heard the words.

Her mind spiralled back to the quiet joy she'd let herself imagine, all born from a few softened words over dinner with her uncle and Sam, dear Sam. Her heart had faltered at the emptiness beside him, and she confirmed her suspicion before he even spoke.

'You've seen her.'

Sam had found Mary, and he had come to tell Emily himself. Mary was alive. He had found her at the protest, and although Mary was elsewhere now – at her lodgings, perhaps, or waiting quietly until this painful conversation was finished – Emily could sense her presence standing invisibly between them.

'Yes. I saw her this morning.' His voice held the same bright wonder she'd longed hearing, but beside her. The wonder faded. 'Emily, I didn't think... it wasn't ever meant to happen like this.'

Her eyes held his for a long time, studying his face like she was memorising it for a test she'd already failed. The words came softer than she intended. 'I think it was always meant to happen like this.'

They stared at each other across the uncharted expanse of the table. Her hands felt light without his. His gaze fell to the full teacup. Emily saw her chance to be the kind of woman she always wanted to be, the kind she'd seen her mother be, the kind that she never thought could hurt so badly to become.

'She is one lucky woman,' Emily said at last. Her eyes flicked back to his. 'Everything you said about her, how important she was to you.' She paused, let her breath catch up. 'I can see it on your face, Sam. You never really believed she was gone.'

He opened his mouth, closed it, looked at her with something close to gratitude and close to pain. 'I thought I could...' He shook his head, tried again. 'You knew about her. I told you about Mary from the start.'

'And you told yourself she wasn't coming back.' Emily bit her lip, watched the colour drain from her words and the air around them. 'When you kissed me, when you smiled... I thought you had finally let her go. But perhaps neither of us ever believed that entirely.'

His hand twitched towards her. She almost moved hers to meet it, stopped herself, pushed the thought away. 'It was always her, wasn't it?'

'No. It was you, too. I wanted to...'

'To forget.' Her mouth gave the ghost of a smile. 'Or not to remember. Maybe that's the same thing.' She looked at him with clear eyes, forced the clouds out of her heart for one brave, kind moment. 'It is all right, you know.'

He shook his head again, harder this time, like a man trying to wake from a dream and the weight of his own guilt. 'Emily, I never wanted to hurt you.'

Her smile held this time, warmed. 'I don't think anyone ever wants that. Not really. Except perhaps Mrs Pettigrew from the bakery across the street.' She gave a light shrug. 'The way she looks at me, you'd think I stole her pie and her sweetheart.'

The attempt at humour hung between them, awkward as a misplaced embrace. Then Sam caught her drift and laughed, a sound more grateful than joyous.

'Thank you for this. For not throwing something at my head.'

'Perhaps next time.' She softened. 'And perhaps you're worth sparing, Sam. Perhaps you're worth quite a bit.'

He met her eyes again, more earnest now, less afraid of what he'd find in them. 'So are you, Emily.' He paused, the words wrestling against some inward grief. 'When I met you, I thought I had nothing left. You reminded me I did. I won't forget that.'

Emily watched him closely, drank in his words with the desperate thirst she used to drink in his affection. 'You're not staying with me because you think you owe me something?'

'No.' He rubbed his face with both hands, an old habit she had always found disarming. 'I didn't know how lost I was until I saw her. Until you made me see.'

'It hurts, but it's the kindest thing you could do for us both. Really, Sam, I want you to be happy.'

'And you? What will you be?'

'Perhaps an old maid. They always have money, I hear.' She smiled again, then faltered. 'Or perhaps a memory for you, as Mary was.'

He looked at her, astonished, wondering how someone could be so unselfish and so piercing all at once. 'I'm sorry. I'm sorry it turned out this way.'

'I'm not,' she said. 'Or at least, I won't be for long. I was hoping it would be us, you know. Really hoping.'

His voice caught, broke. 'I tried. I really did, Emily. I almost convinced myself. Almost convinced you.'

'You almost did. Until Mary. Until she changed every-thing, and nothing, all at once.' Emily sighed. 'You'd better go to her, Sam. Don't leave the poor girl waiting. She's waited long enough.'

His shoulders lifted, as if her goodness had borne away some burden, as if she was an angel instead of a girl he'd nearly fooled. 'I'll always think well of you, Emily.'

'That's more than most people think of me already.'

Sam rose, hesitated, then walked around the table. He paused, unsure if he should reach for her again. Emily lifted her head, and he kissed her softly on the forehead. One final gentle farewell before turning and stepping out into the hallway, back into a world where Mary waited.

Emily watched him go, watched herself in his going, wished for him and wished against herself. Love shouldn't be this way, she thought again, then hated herself for thinking it, for having lost the bravery of her own insistence.

And then it broke, and it was terrible, and it was beautiful, and she was alive again too.

# CHAPTER 22

*M*ary woke up early, letting Sam sleep for another hour before work. She dressed in silence and slipped out just as the first rays of sunshine broke over the rooftops. The familiar ache of Cripplegate squeezed her chest. The area had changed little since the time her mother hung fresh sheets across the lines and her brother crawled under her skirts. She heard it all too clearly – the slap of a hand on a horse's flank, a warning cry of 'Bairn on!' as it skittered across the roadway, and, finally, the whisperings and winks as Mary's father was led away. But she could not think of that. Not now.

A few hours later, she visited Sam at the press. 'I've found him!' Mary's voice trilled with excitement. 'Mrs Wilson's husband. He's still in London! I went back to Cripplegate, to the old lodgings where they used to live beside us. The new tenant knew where they'd gone. He's working at a factory near Bow Road now. He's our witness!'

Sam's eyes lit up. 'You found him!'

'And I know he'll speak. He's got his feet under him now and safe from Turner's reach. We must go to him, Sam.'

'We must, indeed.' He checked the press, reassuring himself the plates were set and ready to run at a moment's notice. 'If he says what you think he will, we'll be a scandal come morning.'

'I know he will. And I'll hold him to it.' A shiver of fear tickled her skin. Her excitement trembled on the edge of hope and panic. It was time, it was nearly time. After all these years.

Sam gave her arm a quick squeeze as if he sensed the tugging at her heart.

He led her past the winding streets teeming with hungry-eyed children. Finally, they reached the doorway of a lodging house where Mrs Wilson's familiar face peered out.

Mary rushed forward. 'I've come to ask something of you.'

'You'd better be quick,' said Mrs Wilson. She frowned, a nervous tick, before ushering them inside. 'It's about your father, isn't it?'

Mary nodded. 'And my mother and little brother. And everything. Is your husband home?'

Mrs Wilson hesitated, the lines on her forehead deepening. 'I'll fetch him.' She disappeared up a stairway, leaving Mary and Sam alone in a bare, cramped room.

'What if he won't?' Mary asked.

'He will.' Sam's voice was firm. 'Even if it takes some convincing.'

Footsteps on the stairs signalled Mr Wilson's arrival. He was a thin, careworn man with the marks of a lifetime of work etched into his face. He looked at Mary with a blend of recognition and unease.

'It's been a long time. You've grown so much,' he said, scratching the back of his neck.

'Far too long. I never thought I'd see you again.'

He looked down at his feet, as if unwilling to meet her eyes. 'What is it you want?'

She took a breath. 'I want the truth. About my father.'

The room fell silent. Mr Wilson glanced at his wife, then at Sam, measuring their intentions.

'Turner is a powerful man,' he said. 'You'd do well to stay out of his way.'

'He's nothing to me,' Mary said. 'Not anymore. And he's not what he once was. We're close to exposing him, but we need your voice.'

Mr Wilson rubbed his chin, the conflict clear in his troubled expression. 'Why would I risk it now? He did me a good turn when my boy was sick.'

'He gave you money. I remember,' Mary said.

He flushed, recalling the tangled web of obligations that had silenced him. 'There was more to it than that,' he confessed. 'Your father. They made him foreman over me, and I...'

Mary stepped forward, her gaze piercing. 'And you let them take him.'

He flinched as if struck, guilt flooding his features. 'I did,' he said. 'I didn't see any other way then.'

Sam's eyes narrowed. 'But there is now. The whole of London will know what kind of man Turner is. You don't have to be afraid.'

Mr Wilson exhaled slowly. 'A foreman at the docks. He had no family here, no one to stand up for him.' His voice was tinged with regret. 'I can't deny it. I saw them setting him up.'

Mary felt a surge of hope. 'Please. If you'll only say it out loud, you could clear his name.'

Mrs Wilson, standing to the side, spoke up. 'For what it's worth, Davey, I think you should help the girl. It's been on your conscience long enough.'

Mr Wilson looked between them, hesitating. Then he seemed to shrink a little, surrendering. 'I'll do it. I'll say it to anyone you like.'

Sam stepped forward, grasping his hand. 'It will make all the difference.'

Mary watched, her heart swelling with a mix of relief and disbelief. Mr Wilson was speaking again, faster now, anxious to unburden himself. 'It was Turner's doing. He was running a racket, getting things stolen on the side and pocketing the profits. He needed someone to take the fall when the overseer came sniffing about, so he planted the goods on Charles. Made it look like he was the one.'

Mary listened, the years of grief and injustice unspooling at last. 'Did you know all along?'

He nodded, shamefaced. 'I knew. But he'd have ruined us back then if I'd opened my mouth. I kept it shut, but I've never felt right about it.'

Sam released Wilson's hand, urgency propelling him towards the door. 'We need to get this written and published before anyone gets wind.'

Mary felt her resolve harden into certainty. 'It's my turn to hold you to your word, Mr Wilson.'

'And I'll keep it. Just get it done quick.'

They were out in the street again. Mary's head spun with the enormity of what they had just accomplished. Sam looked at her, his face alight with purpose.

'This is it, Mary. We've got him now. That crow.'

She wanted to believe him. And she truly did.

They hurried back to Oliver's press, where Sam feverishly wrote out the details of Mr Wilson's testimony, his pen racing across the paper. Mary watched, a hundred emotions churning inside her. When Sam finished, he handed it to her.

'It's ready for tomorrow's edition. Oliver will run it front page.'

Mary's hands trembled as she held the words. Turner Set Bennett Up, Dock Worker Reveals. She stared at it, feeling dizzy with anticipation.

Sam pulled Oliver aside. 'I'll need ten thousand copies. And make it loud.'

The old publisher grinned. 'Trust me, son. They'll hear it clear over at Westminster.'

Mary found herself waiting on a knife-edge between fear and elation. Could it really be so near? After everything? She held the paper as if it might crumble in her hands, her father's name standing boldly against the columns of type.

Oliver nodded towards the door. 'You two look like you could use some air. Let me and the boys take care of things here.'

Sam ushered Mary outside, his arm around her shoulder. 'We did it,' he said. 'We really did.'

The hours crawled by. That night, Mary barely slept, every sound magnified into her waking dreams: the rhythmic thrum of the presses, the shrill whistles of departing trains, the distant hum of the city digesting its morning news. She lay in bed, haunted by shadows of past betrayals and future hope, unable to quell the thoughts that darted like trapped birds in her mind.

Morning came, ushered in by the shouts of newspaper boys hawking their scandalous headlines. Mary and Sam followed the cries, watching as clusters of men and women gathered on the streets, discussing the shocking story. The pages fluttered like a thousand wings, each one spreading the word of Turner's treachery.

Mary felt a thrill of vindication as they moved through

the throngs, seeing the impact of their work in every astonished face. But a kernel of anxiety lodged in her chest, stubbornly refusing to be dislodged.

By noon, the city was in an uproar. Even those who hadn't read the paper heard about it from their neighbours, and the talk was of little else.

Sam and Mary returned to Oliver's, where another stack of papers awaited distribution.

'Never seen it like this,' Oliver said, wiping ink-stained hands on his apron. 'Thought I'd have to beat them off with a stick.'

'Turner will come after us, you know that,' Sam said.

'He can try,' Oliver said with a wink. 'But I've got friends of my own.'

The words were barely out of his mouth when the door swung open, and John Turner stood silhouetted against the midday light. His face was a mask of rage, his voice low and threatening.

'You think you can ruin me with this filth?' he said, holding up a crumpled edition of the paper.

Mary felt a jolt of fear but squared her shoulders, refusing to let it show. 'The truth's out. There's nothing you can do now.'

Turner's eyes burned with a feral intensity. 'You've made a grave mistake. All of you.'

Sam moved in front of Mary, shielding her from Turner's venom. 'Go on, then. See if you scare us.'

Turner tossed the paper to the ground in disgust. 'You'll regret this,' he snarled, then stormed out, leaving the door to slam behind him.

Oliver chuckled, a rich sound full of defiance. 'He looked like a dog what lost its bone.'

The adrenaline had left Mary shaky, and she could feel it in her knees. 'Is it over?'

Sam turned to her. 'It will be. After that little scene, he won't last the day without being brought in.'

Oliver nodded sagely. 'He's right, Mary. Half the East End wants him strung up, and the other half wants a turn with him first.'

The tension of the last twenty-four hours melted away, replaced by an overwhelming sense of relief. Mary laughed, the sound strange and unfamiliar, bubbling up uncontrollably.

'Careful now,' Sam teased. 'Or they'll think you've gone mad.'

She couldn't stop, even if she'd wanted to. The laughter kept coming, mingled with tears of joy and the final letting go of years of hurt.

News of Turner's arrest spread quickly. By evening, the pubs and parlours were buzzing with the tale, exaggerated and embellished with each retelling. Mary and Sam stood on the sidelines, watching the spectacle unfold, feeling the sweet weight of victory.

'I can hardly believe it,' Mary said, her voice still tinged with wonder.

'Believe it. You've done it. It's really over.'

The enormity of their achievement settled on her, filling her with a quiet, profound peace. Her father's name was cleared. The shadows that had haunted her life were finally banished. Her mother and her little angel would be proud.

'What about you?' she asked, searching his face. 'It's as much yours as mine.'

He smiled, the tension of years easing from his features. 'I promised you, didn't I? All those years ago. Right there, next to Tommy. That I'd help you make it right.'

Mary felt a deep swell of gratitude and affection. She had never allowed herself to think they might truly reach this moment. 'I love you, Sam.'

The city bustled around them, its familiar cacophony strangely distant. They stood together, wrapped in the warmth of triumph and the prospect of a future no longer haunted by the past. At last, they were free to imagine what that future might hold.

They walked holding hands in the gathering dusk, knowing that nothing could stand in their way again.

# EPILOGUE

*M*ary found herself at the grand entrance of St Thomas Hospital, clutching a worn carpetbag that had accompanied her through the twists and turns of her young life. Her heart swelled with a mixture of joy and disbelief as she stepped across the threshold, realising she had finally reached the place she had dreamed of since childhood, a place where healing was not merely a wish but a vocation.

She paused to take in the bustling courtyard, filled with nurses in crisp uniforms and doctors engaged in urgent discussions. It was a world of purpose and promise, one that felt as vast and open as her future now seemed. Her thoughts drifted back to that bleak day at Tommy's grave, her whispered vow mingling with memories of his laughter. 'I will do it for you, Tommy,' she had promised him. Today, standing here on the precipice of becoming everything she had hoped to be, she felt that promise echo warmly inside her.

'Turner Sentenced: Workhouse Reforms Promised!' Sam's name blazed beneath the triumphant headline. The exposé had been a strike right into the heart of corruption, and now the justice he had long pursued was unfolding before his eyes. In dimly lit rooms across London, in coffeehouses and chambers where politicians gathered, the impact of his work was being felt.

Oliver slapped him on the back, pride gleaming in his eyes. 'You've done it, lad! You've rattled their cages good and proper,' he said, handing Sam yet another paper that sang his praises. It seemed each new edition held more of Sam's voice, more of his relentless pursuit of truth.

Sam sat amid a whirlwind of change in a small office off Fleet Street, in the very heart of London's publishing world. Letters from hopeful apprentices seeking his guidance piled up at one corner of his desk.

A year later, a gentle snow fell over London, blanketing the city in a hush that made even its busiest streets feel tender and softened. In a small chapel tucked away from the din of Fleet Street, Mary and Sam stood hand in hand, their faces illuminated by the glow of candlelight and the warmth of shared triumphs. The air was alive with joy and the scent of evergreen.

Sam looked at Mary, seeing not just the love of his life but a partner in every battle, every dream he had dared to dream. Her eyes, bright with happiness, reflected his own journey from despair to hope. He squeezed her hand as if to say, we made it, together.

The sight of Lilly among the guests brought a smile to Mary's lips, knowing how defiantly she had come despite Lady Branscombe's disapproval. Beside her sat Oliver, beaming with pride as he watched Sam achieve yet another victory, not just of ink and print, but of the heart.

Sam caught Emily's eye across the aisle. He was delighted to see her smiling back with genuine warmth and sincerity. Their parting had been bittersweet but right; Emily's blessing felt like threads unravelling gracefully where they needed to.

Nellie laughed softly from her seat, nudging Susie as they both glanced at Mary with eyes full of memory and affection. The matchgirls' presence was a reminder of long-ago nights filled with dreams that now bloomed into reality.

As vows were exchanged beneath winter's gentle cloak, it was like sealing every hope they ever held against the chill of adversity, marking each other with a love immune to season or circumstance.

Afterward, gathered under swags of holly and ribbons, Mary's heart soared amid laughter and familiar voices, a chorus that sang not only of today's happiness but also yesterday's resilience. She marvelled at how far they had come. From Cripplegate's walls to this day.

Sam wrapped an arm around her shoulders as Oliver handed him a small parcel tied with string. The old publisher winked knowingly. 'A wedding gift for you both, fresh off our press,' he said while gesturing toward stacks of pamphlets nearby: medical guides for working families that bore not just Sam's investigations but Mary's hard-won knowledge.

Mary opened one carefully and smiled at Sam; this, too, was their creation, a thing meant to mend broken lives beyond even their own spheres.

As dusk settled over the celebration inside the chapel walls, it became clear: this was more than just two hearts entwined. It was an entire world remade through kindness, justice, and unwavering love.

In that tranquil moment when evening gave way to night-fall's embrace outside their new home together, small yet brimming with hope, Mary whispered softly into the deepening quiet: 'We've done it... for everyone.' And there beside her on their first married night stood all that remained, the promise fulfilled, and it shone brighter than any star above London's now-sleeping streets.

**I hope you've enjoyed *The Orphan Nurse*. If you haven't read the FREE prequel *Four Tickets to London*, you can get your copy here:** https://BookHip.com/XTFBMCQ

**You will get to know more about how everything started for the Bennetts as they moved from Ashton to the big city.**

Printed in Great Britain
by Amazon

61590105R00071